T0113345

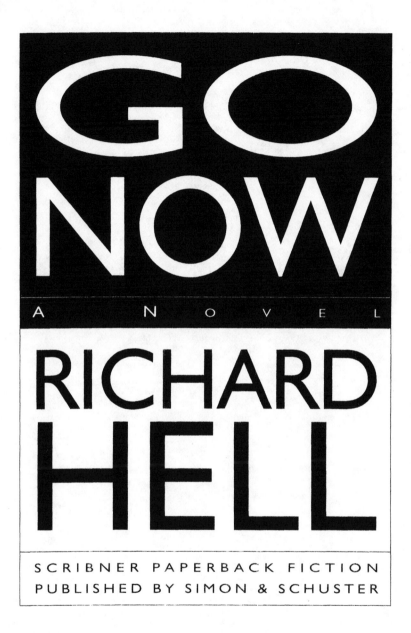

GO NOW

A NOVEL

RICHARD HELL

SCRIBNER PAPERBACK FICTION
PUBLISHED BY SIMON & SCHUSTER

SCRIBNER PAPERBACK FICTION
Simon & Schuster Inc.
Rockefeller Center
1230 Avenue of the Americas
New York, NY 10020

First Scribner Paperback Fiction edition 1997

SCRIBNER PAPERBACK FICTION and design are trademarks of Simon & Schuster Inc.

DESIGNED BY ERICH HOBBING

Text set in Caledonia

Manufactured in the United States of America

1   3   5   7   9   10   8   6   4   2

Library of Congress Cataloging-in-Publication Data is available.

ISBN 0-684-82234-2
0-684-83277-1 (Pbk)

Many thanks to the Rex Foundation.
Portions of *Go Now* were previously published in the following periodicals:
The Portable Lower East Side, Sensitive Skin, Rolling Stone (Australia), *Chelsea Hotel*
(Germany), *Purr* (Great Britain); anthologies: *A Day in the Life* (Autonomedia, NY),
Low Rent (Grove Press, NY), *Jungles D'Ameriques* (AAC, Paris), *AM Lit* (Druckhaus
Galrev, Berlin); and CD reading: *Go Now,* chapters 1 and 2 (CodeX, Great Britain,
and T/K Records). Thanks are given to the editors.

I think of the crowds out there swarming over the streets with their minds clicking and buzzing and yawning with big hopes and schedules and breakfast table slights and anticipations of the boss's reactions and my mind goes blank the way it does when a mathematical problem gets too complicated. I don't get it. I can't reach the strands.

I push the covers off.

I'm alone and I think, that's one good thing about dope, it keeps you conscious that you're alone. Suddenly I want to cry.

I get up naked and in the same motion lift my thick biker's belt from the doorknob beside the bed and slip along the wall into the living room to avoid being seen through the window. I pull loose the loop of string that holds a roll of tattered bamboo halfway up the window and the shade falls with a sharp clatter like a pang of guilt gone in a second. I hang the belt over the back of a chair in front of the couch and go into the kitchen where I fill a glass with water and grab a handful of toilet paper and a plastic bottle of rubbing alcohol. Back in the living room, I put the paper and bottle and water glass on the chair and get my spoon and syringe from a hidden drawer in the table opposite the couch. The spot where I sit on the couch is permanently dented by my weight and radiates a broken fringe of cigarette burns. The spoon, which is black with carbon on the underside, holds a crusty piece of cotton in the middle of a brown stain. The last shot from last night. I suck up some water from the glass with the syringe and squirt it into the spoon. Using the tip of the needle I loosen the cotton and swirl it in the murky liquid to dissolve every last encrusted grain. I light a cluster of five or six paper matches and hold it under the spoon. Get it sterile, make sure it all dissolves. It bubbles, a wisp of steam arises. It clarifies. Everything is focused there. I pull the fluid into the syringe through the filter, press the tube free of air bubbles, and lay it down on the chair. I spin the top off the alcohol bottle, press the toilet paper to the bottle's mouth, upend it, and wipe a path up my left forearm with the fresh-smelling tissue. I tighten the belt around my left bicep and slide the needle into the main vein of the forearm. I push the plunger out with my thumbnail. A thread of blood appears in the liquid. A hit. I loosen the belt. I press the plunger in and yank the needle out.

Fuck. Hardly feel a thing.

Still, I've usefully killed five minutes. Now what?

I erase with the tissue the indifferent bulblet of black-red blood from my badly scarred forearm. I look around.

My apartment's like a cave.

When I was a kid in Kentucky we used to go cave hunting. There are lots of caves there. In the open fields and pastures around the suburb where I grew up you could spot their likely positions by the isolated clumps of trees that rose up from sinkholes where the farmers couldn't plow. We'd take candles and sandwiches and flashlights and go exploring. Get really muddy. Find tiny animal skulls and salamanders. We'd make a fire and cook up plans to run away and hide in the caves, live there, and only appear to civilization as guerrilla marauders, like Jesse James, popping up like hallucinations in supermarkets and raiding unlocked kitchens to pocket some bread and baloney and batteries, running through backyards, caught only for flashes in peripheral vision, escaping back to our dark and soaking hideouts.

There was nothing worse than getting stuck though. The main object of every cave exploration was to find a cavern as big as a room. We never did. But you never knew what a tunnel might lead to. That was the excitement. You'd push yourself inch by inch, crawling, timeless inch-diving through rock on your belly, squirming and squeezing in the chilly darkness, sweat and cave water dripping in your eyes, sharp stone scraping the back of your head, in hopes that the passage would open up like a castle. And then you'd find that you'd pushed yourself in so far that you not only couldn't go further but you couldn't go back. You were wrapped in rock and trapped. Claustrophobic panic would rise like gigantic internal missiles and then either explode or fall down dead. Sometimes the muscle-rockets would blow you far enough backwards to get free. Sometimes you gave up, and that was great for a minute or two, dreaming of rot and revenge with your face in the tiny rivulets. Lovelorn jewels inside your eyelids. Then the fear and desperation would kick in again.

Never thought of that. I reach for a notebook to note the similarities between past and present.

I need to piss. Just got off and I need to piss. That's bad. Means I'll be sick again inside of two hours.

I put away the works. I take a piss and then go into the bedroom and pull on a pair of jockey shorts and a skintight pair of black Levi's that have a couple of nice brown-rimmed holes in the thighs where I hung them too long to dry in the oven one night when I had to play a gig. I button on a tight striped shirt with short frayed cut-off sleeves and pull on a good thick pair of socks that smell all right. Then I carry the phone from beside my bed back into the living room and put it down beside my spot on the couch. I sit there.

I sit there. There's my dick inside my pants, really warm and heavy and potent. Maybe I should jerk off. I haven't come in days—it's like pissing or taking a shit, you can only do it on the outskirts of highs.

The dust is falling. The skeleton pulls out his dick. Whoa. The pleasure, like piercing shards, like pieces of triangles skimming, banging around in your body. Whoa. God, it happens fast when you're straight. Floods of it. And it's practically a convulsion, a little epileptic fit. You almost see stars.

But then it's gone and all that's happened is you're a little emptier, too alert and skinned bare to even drift in the sweetness for more than a minute. Satisfied by slightness, as if you'd eaten too much popcorn. I pull my pants back up and let the feeling wash through me for its allotted time.

The sun is really up now, all the window-coverings in the house are off and I feel overlit. The day is making its demands. Who should I call? Is everybody burnt out? There's always ten dollars somewhere. There's always twenty dollars. Do I have any books worth selling? Should I pawn my guitar again? That's always an option.

It feels a little chilly in here. The spring's the coldest season because the temperature hovers around the level where the slumlords are legally allowed to turn off the heat and they exploit it for all they're worth.

Rrring. All right. My charm's intact. This has to mean at least ten dollars. Anyone who'd call me at this hour must know what they're in for.

It's Chrissa. This is a little delicate. Our relationship runs deeper than is convenient at a moment like this. Still, I know she's solvent and cares about my friendship.

"Chrissa, I was just thinking about you."

"You were? That's nice."

"It is? It is."

"It is."

"What were you calling about?"

"To remind you we are to meet Jack."

"Oh shit. I totally forgot . . ."

"I want to remind you. You don't have nothing to worry about. Jack thinks you're great. He has a plan for you."

She talks a little funny because she's French.

"Yeah, but I don't feel too good today."

"What's wrong?"

"Well, you know, I don't feel too well and I'm flat broke. My refrigerator's a ghost town. It's fuckin demoralizing . . . I just woke up feeling like this, goddamn it, and I'm outta ideas . . ."

"You are hungry?"

"Well, I'm a little hungry. There's some oatmeal . . . I'm not going to starve, but—another day like this?"

"What."

"I'm outta books to sell. I don't wanna pawn my guitar again. I've got rehearsal later and now that Jay down the hall is on the road it'll be hard to find one to borrow. And all cuzza that fucking record company . . ."

"Oh."

"I'm gettin a royalty check from my lawyer next week but he doesn't give advances . . ."

"You want to borrow some money?"

"Could I? If I just had twenty dollars it would be great. I can pay you back as soon as I get that bread from my lawyer next week."

"Don't worry . . . But you're going to be good with Jack, yes? This is important."

"I will. I'll be in top form. I'm going to make it up to you, Chrissa. . . . But listen, actually, do you think you could make it twenty-five, cuz I have a little debt to pay back, too . . ."

"OK, but you have to come over here now since I'm going out."

"I'll be there right away."

I hang up feeling great and slimy at the same time. But soon enough the searing light of my unfailing luck chars the slime to a thin, thin crust, I shrug and stretch, it flakes away, and I'm innocent again. Another eight hours arranged for.

2

Off to Chrissa's. I don't like being outside. I'm afraid there'll be a loud noise and I'll jump. I think how I've lived here so long nothing looks new and interesting anymore. It's hard to find a route where I won't be likely to run into someone I know and realize that they're worried that I'm crazy because of the way I try to force myself to look into their eyes in order to show that I'm not crazy, and then I have to make an abrupt excuse that makes me seem even crazier and move off fast.

I'm a machine that's set to skim, power-walk, to that doorway, collect, and move on to the next. I feel pretty good. It's nice to be seeing Chrissa too. I haven't seen much of her for awhile. It's ugly that right off I'm borrowing money from her, but she doesn't seem to mind. She can afford it. I'll make it up to her when I get paid. Something like, um, a champagne and caviar dinner. Or better yet a trip to the country—with me. I bet that she could still love me. I don't want to think about how I feel about her. I bounce off that place like a superball. For now she's twenty-five bucks. I love her breasts. I love her ass—her butt . . . her rear end. There's no good word for that place. I'd like to ski off it. Or would she smile me away? Just thinking about it makes me feel cute. I hate it when she makes me feel cute.

She knows me too well. I've had to apologize too often. I've confessed too much. And made the wrong confessions. She's seen my resolve fail too many times.

Why am I going on like this? Am I a broken man? I laugh, and a passerby glances at me and instantly looks away.

Springtime: not hot enough for the garbage to smell. These old people with their dogs are ridiculous. How could someone let himself get old and wander around with a fleabit hound on this vicious battleground? Well, they're just wallpaper to me. But this existence needs some redecoration.

Then again, nothing ever changes. I can just imagine I'm a time traveler and it all becomes interesting again. Where am I? I walk down Tenth Street where proud Puerto Ricans—after all, they've survived to be teenagers and are making money at a good clip—exchange little ticket-size envelopes of marijuana for five dollarses. Out in the sun like that the money always looks like it has a silver patina you could smudge with a thumb. As if it were magic, and if everybody would stop pretending the stuff would just disintegrate.

I remember having a little epiphany, a little insight into the timeless state of things once when I was walking alone on Fourteenth Street, where everything looks medieval anyway. I saw everyone in the dignity of their fate, their origin, their condition: each one a separate manifestation of the earth's possibilities, each person another something spoken by the world. But now I'm thinking the race is nearing its death and it's going to realize that its efforts to fathom the universe and fulfill itself, the patterns it has created in striving for knowledge, beauty, and harmony—riches and world domination—all merely add up to a self-portrait, and it's an ugly, brutal, selfish face. The more lines that are added to the face of the earth the more detailed and clear the subject of the portrait becomes, as we near our finish, and soon the world will erase us and return to the drawing board. Maybe dinosaurs'll get another chance.

Chrissa lives on the top floor of a building on St. Mark's Place. It shocks me mildly to see how I can resent her for forcing me to climb seven flights of stairs to borrow twenty-five dollars from her.

I get up there and she's sitting in the middle of the floor thumbing through a single-drawer file cabinet. A glance at her does two things: It makes me glad to be alive, and makes me feel left behind and shut out of life altogether. Damn damn damn. I hate this real life where actual people with their own desires and intentions can look at me, expect things of me, interpret my behavior, classify me. I prefer my mental life where Chrissa and

I are together forever the moment we locked eyes five years ago.

How did I get to be old enough to say "five years ago"? If I can get to twenty-nine I can get to forty. I've been wondering about this.

"Hi Chrissa, whatcha doin?"

"Looking for some pictures for a job I got."

"Oh . . . You know, I was just thinking about something. I read somewhere recently that the Greeks thought of the past as being ahead of them and the future behind. You know, because the past is what you actually see, it's what you know, what you're really facing, whereas the future . . . it's wherever your back is turned. And anyway, it's mostly made outta the past. Kind of comforting, don't you think?"

"Yes, I know you'd really like to make your future behind you."

"Don't be mean now. Don't be cruel."

"There's your money over there. I know you're in a hurry."

"You know, those Greeks . . . how did they get to be so philosophical? It must be because they made up the word. But gee, it seems like they saw the big picture all the time. It must have been because of their gods. When all we have are movie stars. See, their gods were like people, while we've degenerated into treating people like gods. Can you imagine if Liza Minnelli or Al Green or Clint Eastwood could turn you into a duck? That would make you philosophical."

She laughs. Wow. That's good luck. I still have a little juice. I can get out of here on a good note.

But this is just a stop on my dope run and to whatever degree she knows or acknowledges she knows that, it's enough to make her despise me a little, with regret. This flaw in the moment is like a secret vanity of mine she's discovered, as if she's caught me posing in the mirror kissing myself, and it only makes me want to leave sooner.

"I would be a duck for Al Green," she says, "but our god of now is Jack and for some twisted reason of his he has a special fondness for you, which for all of us I hope you appreciate. I don't know how much more chances you're going to get—I admit you always seem to find another—but I'm involved in this too . . ."

She sure can get cold. She isn't giving me an inch. Well, it's only sensible. I pick up the money.

"See you," I say, and then, "I'm going to come through, Chrissa. I know you're right. Whatever this plan Jack has, if you think it's so interesting, it must be worthwhile. I'll be there today and I'll be in good shape."

I make her stand up and hug me before I leave.

Back to the street, where I am King. Lord of the garbage. I go to cop.

Copping is about as interesting as waiting for a subway train. Nothing good can happen—there's never a pleasant surprise—it's just a monotony that always has the potential of turning into something worse.

I go on automatic again, pacing the most efficient route at a steady high speed sufficient to discourage all but the stupidest or craziest passersby from thinking they might be free to detain me. I'm on important business. I know how to walk mean, with an expression of intimidating determination that's by you before you've recovered enough to jump it, friend or foe.

I cop the dope and the trip home is a breeze. I am set free—nothing can shake me except for the reflexive anxiety that pushes my fingers into the watchpocket of my jeans every couple of blocks to make sure the bags can't get dislodged. I feel like school is out. There is nothing else in the world I need.

I leap up the stairs to my apartment and have my shirt off before I get to the living room. I assemble my paraphernalia with a speed, precision of movement, and conservation of energy the equal of the finest mystic craftsmen of old. A tea ceremony of sorts.

In a moment I'm high. The silence and inching shadows in my room are very beautiful when resonant with heroin, all anxiety dissolved. My writhing ceases. I am competent, I am good, I'm in tune.

I have my notebook beside me, a sixteen-ounce bottle of Coke, and a bag of peanuts.

I'm a ticker-tape machine of poetry, an acrobat of spiritual language who even feigns slips for the hair-raising grace and hilarity of my recoveries for God alone. God being all the dead poets. All and everything. The watcher who grows and branches and forgives me while hoping for the best. Me dreaming the world in my own image where it radiates from my empty room where I'm alone and happy.

I pick up a magazine and by total "coincidence"—one sees what one is alert to—read, "There is no I . . . there is only God. It is He who glistens on the ocean's surface amid the orange groves; the heady fragrance is also He, and so is the wind, the snake, the shark, the wine. Do not see yourself as yet another dream; go on dreaming yourself."

The guy must be Mediterranean. Somewhat overbiblical, plus he's a little lacking in the shark department, but that last line has a good twist. I set to dreaming.

I shake my head and the tiny acrobats fall like spangles, like the cool rain on another planet, down to the inside of my feet.

I have to pull myself together. It's almost time to meet Jack.

3

Jack is British and he doesn't reveal much that's personal about himself. This puts me at a disadvantage because I tend to confess. I don't know why I do that. I guess it's because I think that everyone's capable of anything and the trouble is that no one'll admit it . . . And then there's the way that things that scare you when you keep them to yourself just seem scientifically interesting when you say them out loud. Plus, I have hardly anyone else to talk about.

Anyway, he doesn't reciprocate, but since I'm so frank he'll start acting like we're brothers, which is annoying because I don't really know him. I go along with it, though, because he keeps doing things for me. He's got a lot of money from managing a string of speed-freak alcoholic British groups. I don't really have much in common with him or his sotted crew, but his deference is flattering. Still, I have a running anxiety that I'll talk too much some time and one gruesome quip'll snap him aghast and I'll never see him again.

My work is a sort of con game in these situations. I'm selling my confidence. The uncertain buyer wants to identify with you. Jack thinks I'm the real article, and he wants a spiritual piece of it. He thinks I'm some kind of shred of soul from his second-hand dream of big true-hearted America, a radiant dark slider through the open-spaced underworld of his long-gone U.S., honest rock & roll on the radio. I don't have to tell him there's a swollen trough of scab extending from the wrist to inside-elbow of the arm that holds the wheel, while the middle finger of the other is stuck in my ass, and a naked hard-on thrusts up between them, throbbing me wacky till I could die or kill, or fuck his wife in a second. Maybe he even knows it already. He does know a lot.

I call him from the desk of the Gramercy Park Hotel.

"Come on up, you egotestical old fart."

Right off, though I know he's smiling, my reaction is that he doesn't know me well enough to talk to me like that, and neither does anyone else. Then I realize he's made a pun and I'm impressed, along with a condescending little rush of affection because he's trying to communicate with me.

Upstairs I find Chrissa with him, basking in it. I wonder if they've been having sex. That would feel horrible so I don't think about it. Jack has a predilection for cocaine, which puts the strain of another unasked question—where's mine?—on the situation.

He's a tallish footballer at thirty-four, wearing a greasy ducktail and dressed in a vaguely rockabilly-style mohair suit and thin tie. He's quick and articulate, though he looks like a tough city limey.

He's all right, but I'd rather not see Chrissa serving herself up to him like it's inevitable. As far as she'll bend backward to disguise it she's susceptible to the flatteries of stardom, and that pains me and taints her a little in my feelings.

It turns out he wants to take me to lunch in the restaurant downstairs and when we all arrive in the lobby, he sends Chrissa home. That's good—I don't want everything all scrambled by the distracting signals she keeps sending off.

The two of us take window seats at a table in the bar and he asks me how I am and what I've been up to.

I order a double scotch to help gather my resources, consolidate them there in the dim Gramercy Park bar, in a chair at the window, facing this ruddy shining face that's directed at me like a spotlight.

My recent life has been so solitary that it sounds to me as if my voice is rusty, and that I might have lost control of its automatic volume monitor as well, and I'll have to step in and regulate it consciously.

I'm also a little disoriented by my uncertainty about Jack's conception of me, as if I'm auditioning for a role that's never been fully described to me. I wish I had a better idea of who I was supposed to be being.

I tell him I'm drinking a lot, that I'm demoralized by how the negotiations to get myself free from my record company are dragging on while keeping me from recording anything new, etc., etc. I kid him a little and inquire about his empire.

He kids me back and impresses me with his current doings. Then he talks about Chrissa, how he admires her and regrets that she doesn't get the respect she deserves as a photographer. I let him know I appreciate her as much as he does. We eat sandwiches. I feel him looking at me from behind his eyes. It isn't that he's assessing me coldly, but that he's as aware as I am of the necessity for continuous vigilance.

"Jack, Jack, Jack, Jack," I say, fumbling for position.

"So how are you?" he asks. "Keeping the nurses jumping?" He refers to any girl who'll return my call as a nurse.

"The nurse pageant continues, but I'm someplace else. I've got a lot on my mind."

"A vacant lot!"

"Oh, Christ, oh no—you're making word plays now?" Or maybe I've forgotten or never noticed.

"Are you off smack?"

"Yeah. I've finally gotten really clean. It took me over a year of refining the method, switching back and forth between dope and methadone. You know, what it is is they each block the need for the other, but they're both addictive, so you have to switch back and forth, lowering the doses, stopping one before you get a bad habit and then going back to the other, needing less of it, till finally you're clean. But it's left my life a wreck. I need a project to really apply myself to."

"That's what I want to talk to you about."

"Yeah, I had kind of been given that idea."

"I might have something you'd enjoy doing that could make us both a little money. I have a car in Venice, California, I'd like you to drive back here to New York. All expenses paid, of course. It's a fire-colored '57 DeSoto Adventurer. You can take as long as you want driving . . . It's what happens on the way I'm interested in. I want to know what you see, I want you to look for something, and I want Chrissa to go along. She'll take pictures, you'll write. What do you think of that?"

"What color of fire?"

"Orange fire," he says a little wearily. "Some punter got clever. It should be gold and white. I'll probably repaint it."

I have to think for a minute—every sentence he's saying is another surprise. I keep a poker face though.

"DeSoto Adventurer . . . That's a little lurid, isn't it? Sounds interesting. . . . Nuclear aftermath kind of fire, I bet. . . . Sounds very interesting. . . . But what am I supposed to look for?"

"You're the poet. You figure it out. You're a writer, man. We'll put it to some *use*. Seein you can't make a record because of that idiotic coke-head bastard, we'll make a book and hurt all the way to the bank. Then I'll sell it to the movies!"

It sounds good, though it's all too complex—the picture of me he's superimposing on me, which I'm trying to lip-sync to; the real excitement I feel about his offer undermined by the doubt that I'll ever be comfortable away from my green couch, over-ridden by the intense desire to shake off the cobwebs and prove what I can do . . . He's caught me off guard.

I stall for a few moments longer, asking some broad questions. (When do we go? Soon.) He'll be in touch with Chrissa about the financing. Basically, I don't want to ask too much, out of fear I'll limit my options or he'll lose confidence in me. Anyway, I want to go home. I thank him, make some excuses, and I'm out the door.

4

Wow. It's happened again. My unfailing luck. I bump through the revolving doors of the small hotel and into the open like a little boy whose fifth grade teacher has just tongue-kissed him. I feel my happiness condensing behind my Adam's apple and inside my eyes, releasing little pin-point particles that fizz and pop and bounce around inside my body. It's like I've been touched by a wand. Unbelievable. I have it. It still works. I'm alive with the good witch, naked, in a big bubble of it floating down Lexington Avenue. New York, my own blurry theme park, has never seemed so kind and sustaining. My throat opens up, my eyes tear over, and I can't wait to talk to Chrissa about it.

There's a tiny monkey grip of intimation that this isn't entirely a gift, that ultimately it's an obligation that'll require a lot from me, but I shrug it off before it can scare me, cuz I got a right. The King He lives. And I am Him. I am Him.

Not only that, I know I can turn it into cash today, one way or another.

Like an idiot, I'm still nursing my delirium when I get back to the cave. The light on the answering machine is blinking. I play back the tape.

A totally affected "sultry" purr: "Hi Billy, it's Meredith, and I'm wet wet wet with the need for another lesson. Today. Whatever you say. Call me, please. Pleeease."

When it rains it pours. I'll call her in a few minutes, but I have to try Chrissa first. I drop down on the dusty green couch and dial.

"Hello," she says.

"My, my, my . . ."

"Well, what you think of it, Billy?"

"It's too soon to think. I just want to . . . revel. Wanna revel?"

"Way, pretty good isn't it?"

"I tell ya, I was startin to lose faith. This is just what I need. I gotta hand it to the guy."

"He's a genius, as much I hate him. You know what the money thing is?"

"Kind of, but tell me."

"We both—I mean we each—get fifty dollars a day for expenses and then we get his credit card for the gas and motels."

"My God—how are we supposed to get any work done?"

"Really," she laughs.

"Well, but I guess whatever we do is work. I mean it seems like he just wants us to . . . go through it, and just keep track of what happens. The real work comes later, right?"

"I guess so—your part of it. I must take pictures."

"Well, I'll have to be taking notes. Writing down what happens. But what are we really looking for exactly? Do you have a handle on that?"

"You don't know? He didn't talk it with you?"

"Not really. He wasn't very . . . forthcoming that way. He wasn't specific at all."

"Well, I guess he's trusting you."

"Oh, great. Chrissa, I'd sure like to talk to you about all this. Can I come over later?"

"Sure. I'm gonna be here all day."

"Good. It probably won't be till eight or nine. Is that OK?"

"Uh huh. I think so."

"I'll talk to you then."

"Fine."

"Bye."

Mmmmm. I'm still too lightheaded. It's always dumb to get excited. Meredith'll cool me out.

Creaky voice: *I am the scientist of my moods. I. Observe. Myself. Microscopically.* But it looks like . . . nothing's there . . . so

. . . I apply calculated doses of . . . sexual heat and drug tint . . . to give me substance, make me visible, while disturbing my being as little as possible. I writhe and shudder with the effects of my handiwork beneath the microscope, thinking it must be God's work. I am nothing and I am God, therefore. . . . How'd it come to this?

Never mind.

Meredith could cool me out.

In the little world of dingy nightclubs where I make my living, the girls, as a rule, are there to be abused. They judge the musicians' importance and desirability by how freely the guys'll use them. At the same time they're grateful for the smallest kindness, as long as it's the exception. Rock & roll is a lot like pimping. The object is to make insecure young girls willing to pay money to be near you.

Merry first called me three or four years ago, when she was fourteen. She'd tried to sound suave on the phone, asking to interview me for her school paper, but she laughed too suddenly and made the most crudely suggestive promises. In fact we recognized each other immediately, like Joan Crawford and George Sanders. She'd brought a girlfriend on her first visit but she's come alone ever since.

She's a plump, precocious, black schoolgirl, pretty and provocative in her short dark kilt, kneesocks, and crisp white blouse. She unbuttons the blouse to the bottom of her bra the minute school lets out.

She'll do anything for me. She's even developed an ingenious little charade to replace the travesty of my "borrowing"s of ten dollars to go cop whenever she arrives. She asked to be allowed to give me ten dollars a minute for criticizing her technique as she tries to mouth and squeeze my penis to orgasm. I sit on the couch and she gets down on her knees between my legs. She calls me Teacher. Unfortunately, she's never improved. The sessions remind me of how when I was a kid I tried pushing live mice into my pubic hair.

So I call her.

She comes over.

She chirps and drawls at me in this flirtatious, conspiratorial style I know is as thin and fragile as old film stock. Everything is coy sex, or else gossip and name-dropping. It makes me impatient because it's so offensively pitiful, but I just channel my irritation into coldness and mockery and she laps it up, reaching new depths of precious self-abasement for my benefit. I don't really like the way I intimidate her, but I keep seeing her because she is everything I've asked for.

We perform our moment in my ruined living room and bedroom, the windows dusty and marbled like carriers of some skin disease, the eternally intrusive light penetrating them nevertheless, in grimy shafts, capturing our movements in sequential friezes, frozen there in dead ritual, as if we're tarnished bronze, mottled with a powdery pale green dinge that smears ourselves as we touch. Like crude half-humans only partly emerged from the walls and furniture. A dream come true. Her vagina looks so pink and mushy, so liquid and glossy, though, and my cock so drained and massive piercing it there in the container of her chocolate skin. A real valentine of human space.

Her capacity for deflecting my verbal assaults with lame but indomitably persistent simulations of worldly repartee, and for embracing and even embellishing upon the casual sexual abuse to which I subject her, always amazes me. But her pretense to some sad third-hand conception of sophistication drives me to such lengths of frustrated viciousness that the honest life in her rises up unexpectedly from unknown human depths, rendering the clumsy writer a self-satisfied moron, his tale grotesque and artificial. Unless you're really smart and point it out like me.

Time to pray.

One of the gifts of my condition is a detachment that makes my timing impeccable: I tell her it's time to go and she leaves.

Rehearsal is at seven. It's now almost six. I don't really feel much like going. I decide to call Jim. He's the only guy remaining in the band I still feel any responsibility toward.

25

"Oh, Copley," I moan, "I'm very, very tired."

"You don't wanna rehearse?"

"Did I say that?"

"Let me put it this way: I feel certain I detect beneath your tedious whine the intention to cancel rehearsal tonight."

"Gee, that's perceptive. Maybe you're right. It's probably important that I pay attention to my submerged feelings. Any objections?"

"Would I miss an opportunity to stay home and vilify your corpse?"

"You're not really pissed off, are you?"

"I think I'll leave you guessing about that."

"I doubt it."

"Listen, I've got plenty of other things to do. Or maybe I'll call up Stiv Bators and have him come over to the studio as long as you can't make it."

I laugh.

"Copley, you're the funniest guy I ever met. You know, Merry was just over here. You know who I'm talking about, right?"

"Your little student?"

"Yeah—"

"No wonder you're tired."

"You know what she asked me this time? She asked me if it was true that you'd 'accidentally' killed a ten-year-old girl once."

"*What?*"

"I swear. It must come from something you said backstage sometime. I just laughed and laughed, and Merry sat there looking at me with these big, slightly confused eyes. Sometimes I worry about her."

"Yeah, when you're not too busy injecting semen into her rectum."

"Hey—that's not true. She's a very sweet person."

"Mmm hmm, and not only that, but when you're done you can just press the air out of her and put her in your closet."

"I told her that dead girl wasn't entirely an 'accident.'"

"What? You did? Did you really? You could have. But I know you didn't. Did you?—"

"Nah."

"Well, are we rehearsing or not?"

"Um . . . let's leave it up to fate. You call Tom and Larry and I'll call Mark and if they haven't already left we'll cancel it. Next rehearsal's on Thursday."

"All right."

We reach the guys and I get my wish.

5

I didn't break it to him about my trip because he'd be pissed off that I'm neglecting the band. The group is a pretty crippled entity as it is. I've basically lost interest in it. I'm the leader, it's my band, but basically I'm occupied elsewhere. I can camouflage my indifference in the general pessimism and disgust I have in common with him, but even that is wearing thin with Copley. Nevertheless, I take it for granted that he'll have to live with my choices, because if he can't I don't care.

I'm glad to have a few hours alone before I go to see Chrissa. There's never any problem figuring out what to do as long as I'm high. Junk is like an orgasm stretched in time. You just want to surrender to the thick waves of glinting pleasure and luxurious well-being that come like caresses from within, weighing down your eyelids and even, at times, washing forth erotic little moans in the silence. Anything that interferes by demanding attention is annoying. I rarely even answer the phone for the 23 hours a day I'm high.

But then, of course, it turns out the more you need something the less good it does you. I wasn't entirely lying to Jack—I've spent this whole last year systematically attempting to overcome my habit, but three days is tops. Three days deserves a celebration and the only celebration is getting high.

Mostly I just pretend it isn't happening and that I've chosen my way of life on purpose. After all, I'm always only two weeks away from being fine. Now, with the new project looming, my plan is to cop some methadone, clean up, and let the job lead me back to health.

*

I pick up my notebook, feeling suddenly captured by the recollection of a memory I had out on the streets this afternoon walking to Gramercy Park.

Memories are better than life. Nothing I'm part of is good until later. I love what time does. I make decisions on the basis of sensing what will produce the best memory. They're my finest works: all that multidimensional and liquid maze of experience minus the fear and uncertainty, or with the fear and uncertainty changed to something else. Because they are already finished. I've made them up and they comprise me. It's as if experience is only the dark, chaotic factory where these little infinity jewels are pressed into being. Everyone is the poet of their memories. Usually it's better to get things over with so you have the memory. But like the best poems, they're also never really finished because they gain new meanings as time reveals them in different lights. Maybe every memory is inside you from the beginning; they erupt and branch and merge in fantastic patterns, but if you really tried you could trace any one of them back to the same original. Maybe the best ones are all the same: of being born. Or dying, or whatever it is.

The memory I had this afternoon was mixed up with the season and weather itself, like a secretion of that tangle. It returned me to the age of nineteen, still feeling newborn on the Lower East Side with my friend Mick. We were alone in New York then, immigrants from the sticks, deranged by our unknown brilliance. Our inflamed energies overwhelmed us and alternately burnt us into ennui. But when winter ended all that writhing subsided in the arrival of the day when you could throw the windows completely open for the first time in months and it felt like everything was possible. No, it was a feeling that even preceded "everything is possible." It was the feeling that nothing is necessary, nothing is required: Here, it is all given to you. And given to all of you. And everyone can just enter and drift with it. There's nothing more that you have to do, and everything is waiting. It has arrived. The secret dreams are true.

The rim of spring seems to always take me back to those particular years and that place and that friend. The pervading sense is of walking on Second Avenue near St. Mark's Church in 1971 or so, under a blue sky on one of the first days when you could go out without your winter coat, probably on the way to a bookstore on St. Mark's Place, and I'm smiling a little, looking upward, gesturing, and utterly untied. One day we spent half the afternoon fertilizing the parking meters on Eighth Street. We'd do figure eights among them, flapping our bent elbows while humming a buzz and nuzzling our cheeks to every post within half a block. Or we spent all day going from dusty bookstore to dusty bookstore among the shelves and shelves of old used books on Fourth Avenue, searching for French poets. Or sit in the empty white railroad apartment on Eleventh Street where we spent most of our time, taunting and provoking each other, listening to music, and reading or writing, with maybe a stick of incense burning, the curtains billowing slowly inward. We were phased by a nameless dissatisfied restlessness that felt nearly crazy but could overflow into the headiest acts. Like the time we pushed our leaky refrigerator that the landlord would never repair out the fifth-floor window, or the outrageous poems we wrote together.

This afternoon the early spring in New York returned me to that time and place again for the barest moment and I'm grateful. It isn't gone and it never will be, nor will anything else. No matter what I've done to myself, soon it will be a memory, and all memories are good.

It's darkening out now. Pretty soon I should take a bath and get over to Chrissa's. I go into the kitchen and get the bathwater running. *Clank, clank, crunch:* convulsive rusty spurts increasing to a steady violent spew that gradually clears. As in most of the tenements on the Lower East Side, my bathtub sits exposed in the kitchen. This is because the place had originally been built with no more plumbing than the sink, and when the toilet and tub were connected up to the pipes there was only just enough room left in the tiny kitchen to seal off the commode. All three—toilet, sink, and tub—are clustered with the pipes along the wall opposite the apartment's entrance. The large window over the sink gives a different angle into the same airshaft between buildings that the living room window faces. But god-damnit, there's no hot water again. Fucking landlord. Should I heat some on the stove or skip it? I'm not that dirty. I undo a couple of buttons, pull my shirt over my head, wet, soap, and rinse my face in the lukewarm water, mop and rinse my underarms, and then push down my pants, pressing my thighs against the curled white lip of the tub, and thoroughly swab my dick and asshole in case Chrissa gets sentimental or coke-crazed. Though I'm a little sorry to remove the last residue of Merry altogether. I like the smell, if not the stickiness, and removing it, especially with these ulterior motives, feels a little like insulting someone who's just died. Or as if I were a prostitute. I wonder where she might be right this minute. Don't want to pursue *that* idle query around too many corners. I am a whore. No, *she* is. Neither of us are. Everyone is. That'll do. I feel practically clean.

Refreshed, I return to my couch. Thank God for small favors, my mother used to always say. In fact, I feel blessed: all my needs taken care of for weeks ahead. I should consider what I have to discuss with Chrissa.

The truth is, none of it seems real. Even as I consider it—the "facts" of my sudden good fortune—I feel two-dimensional. As if I've won the lottery. Dislocated, disoriented, and a little contaminated. Hmmm, best jump off that train of thought as well. It'll pass: let it. Somehow, I know, the whole world is a construction of one's own state of mind, but it's not so extreme: There are true conditions, there is an environment, too. Reality is the interplay. Stop thinking. Relax.

Outside the darkness is coming down. The magic feels cold. But in my veins runs the blood of reptiles; I am a still, blinking lizard camouflaged among the dusk, gazing, my temperature and activity rate slowly conforming to the environment. Alone and motionless in the deepening dimness. What do I suddenly want to leap to cling to? What is the impulse? Why make the exertion? At best, all roads lead back to this room. Well, I suppose in this life all there is to do is play the game as if it mattered. It doesn't matter that it doesn't matter. Hot-toe-mitey.

6

I've known her since 1975 when she first briefly visited New York from France. She hardly spoke English at all. She was seventeen and I was twenty-four.

In the course of the three weeks she first spent here, she'd moved me and removed me and then moved into me, leaving me gasping—I can still feel it in my stomach when I think about it—like I was the invaded victim in a space parasite movie, as if my heart and lungs were furniture she might be throwing out but would certainly rearrange at whim. She seemed to come from another dimension.

She was little, with matted hair. She had—she has—a square jaw and these big marshy lips. Eyes like drains, like reality drains, like in *Psycho* where Janet Leigh's blood whirlpools away down the tub along with everything else in the movie. Her nose is flat, her whole face is flat. A slim body, nearly hipless, but with bookshelf buttocks and largish uptilted breasts, the kind with nipples that look like just little ticks of pale paint.

She was a spectacle: carnivore and prey in one, like a walking wildlife film, with that riveting amoral charisma of nature. A complete mystery. At seventeen, she was more sophisticated than anyone I'd ever known, while also seeming utterly unaffected. Or at least her affectations came from such a stubborn confidence and will to defy convention that they were irresistible.

She said she'd fallen in love with me, but it went unconsummated. She'd come to New York with her boyfriend, who was even older than me, and I was also involved with someone else. I didn't know what her point was but the pain of want was almost enjoyable. We splurged a few kisses, the promises of which kept us half-disturbed nearly all the time we were together, and we once spent an entire night fully dressed in bed simply holding hands.

I'll never forget the smell of the sparklingly fresh men's white dress shirt that she wore that night, and the lush molecular lamina of her sweat that underlay it, barely, like faintly toxic frayed silk, as dead-end transporting as a child singing to itself. She slept; I didn't. It was one of the most intense nights of love I've ever known.

She left me crazed and bewildered. The night after she returned to Paris I found myself lying alone in bed holding my own hand pretending it was hers.

I didn't see her again for nearly two years. I thought about her though, and wrote her long letters, eventually enclosing press clippings as the band I was in started making waves. She'd send me envelopes bulky with two or three funny and exquisite postcards as well as little swatches of sumptuous fabric or leaves or glossy strange images from art and fashion magazines. She was always traveling.

When she returned to New York, I was a little more accomplished and self-sufficient and she was more interested in pleasing me. The balance had shifted: I was still her captive but my confidence had grown and I'd learned that by rearranging my nerves and emotions—from the inside or out—I could survive her torture, and though her willfulness still upset my expectations, she made greater efforts to console and keep me. My achievements in the intervening months had made me more desirable to her. I was becoming dominant in my territory and she responded to it.

But I had begun my slide. I tended to withdraw to my cave when my responses were damaged and I was preoccupied by my drug intake, but she spent many hours with me here. The sustained dark euphoria of those nights was too innocent to be merely sordid. We each fed the other's most secret strengths and leanings, whole private dream-mythologies of ourselves that had been latent or stunted by neglect until we alone allowed them in each other. We photographed each other in the artificial light at four A.M. and then invented sex in the washed-out music of those hours and fell asleep as the dawn arose. We read books together, we wrote poems and made drawings. One night we pissed on each other. Everything took place in stills and slow motion, grainy black and white, as we lived out our intimate mutual filament of what was possible and desirable in this world.

We didn't talk a lot. Though her English improved quickly, she was French and we had very few common references. Time and again we could not make ourselves understood to each other on any level, from the most mundane reference to popular culture to the most piercing (mis)understandings of the acceptable ground rules between lovers. On good days we would live exclusively on the idyllic small islands of common ground above those complicated oceans. At other times one of us would nearly drown trying to reach the other across the expanses of collapsing surface. Tears and violence.

Bizarrely, that original French boyfriend had come to New York with her again and she remained linked to him the entire time. It was this that tormented me the most and often served as the excuse for another dose of junk. The ironic thing was that he was a devoted admirer of mine. In his own country he was capable and powerful—the entrepreneur owner of a small chain of chic clothing stores for the young, and publisher of the smartest French rock & roll magazine—but in America he was at a loss and relied on Chrissa to protect and guide him. The most I could make out of it was that she felt responsible for him here and that he payed her bills. It was hard for me to take, but then *I* didn't want to pay her bills.

Over the years since then, as we both traveled for work and as my self-debauchery and disillusion took me down, things changed between us. Our lives separated. This happened simply because no one took the trouble to prevent it. To tell the truth I can hardly remember how it faded. All that period when I was touring and resolutely despoiling myself is a haze. I know I hurt her. She didn't judge me, but she was disappointed in how I behaved. It was something we didn't talk about directly.

*

7

She travels so much that she hardly ever lives in an apartment for more than a few months. They're always new and bare. Even though she's been in the place on St. Mark's Place a while it hasn't gotten cluttered. It's a railroad flat: four small rooms falling straight back from her windows overlooking the street—bedroom, living room, kitchen, darkroom. The pale wood floors are fresh with polish and the apartment looks both bright and dark. The scent of her toiletries half wakens its own sense of pleasure now and then, like mama's milk. The unmatched curtains on the windows and the few scarves and items of her clothing strewn around are more like highlights than mess. It's so unlike what my place has become I feel like an intruder at first.

When I open her door she's bent in a red canvas director's chair at a low table covered with pretty junk: a French composition book, some costume jewelry, a half-filled wine glass, 8 x 10 photos, some pastel paper. She's holding a fountain pen. She makes a mark on one of the lined pieces of paper and comes over and hugs me.

"Hi Mister."

"Howdy, Ma'am."

"Want a glass of wine?"

"Sure." The wine bottle and an extra glass are on a half-height partition between the bedroom and the living room. The black brushed-steel boom box beside them is playing some kind of over-produced slow dance soul at a low volume.

I take the glass of red wine she hands me and walk around the room looking at the mostly familiar pictures. I like it that there are a couple of me.

"What's this?" It's a color photo of two gaudily dressed

37

women walking toward the camera in the middle of an empty New York street.

"I just like what is happening with the light. I got it from one of those," she says, pointing to a small stack of thick fashion magazines in a corner.

I see what she means about the picture. The sun is going down at the end of the street and the clouds around it are blue and purple rimmed with pink. The light is almost gone but still in the foreground the meager flesh and faces and greeny satin clothes of the women striding toward us glow with whiteness.

"I see what you mean. It couldn't happen, could it?"

"I know how to do it."

"You figured it out?"

"Yeah. It's nothing really. The problem is it's color and I don't know much about color, but I'm learning."

"You're always learning."

"Aren't you?"

"Well, I'm learning how little I know."

"That's higher learning."

"Higher's my specialty."

"Ain't it the truth . . ."

Uh huh. It sounds so cool when she uses American expressions.

Apart from the bright canvas chair, the table, and a small file cabinet, there are only a couple of thin rugs and fat pillows on the floor. I sit on a rug against the wall.

"It's nice in here."

"Oh, you are such a charming guest."

"Good launching pad for our adventure."

"You have been thinking about it?"

"Not exactly."

"You haven't?"

She's gone into the front room. I can see across the partition that she's rummaging in a little carrying case.

"Well, I've got a few ideas, but mostly I've just been grooving on it. It feels so good to have something to . . . apply myself to. I know we can do a great job. And won't it be fun? It's like a miracle . . ."

"Isn't it? That's just what I was thinking." She comes back and sits in the chair. "It actually is like he's God. Reached down to deliver us. . . . If we can handle it. I'm wondering if he likes to play chess with us." She's tapping cocaine from a tiny brown jar onto the cover of her composition book.

"I'm not that interested in his motives. I think you're much more fascinated by the guy than I am."

"That's predictable."

"What—that I would think it, or that it's the case?"

". . . Both."

". . . I don't wanna argue."

"Neither do I."

She offers me the book and a cut-down straw. I take them and pass the yellow-white ridges of stuff under my face and the fumes have that glittering cat-piss smell that has my heart pounding already. I put the book on the floor in front of me, bend over it, and snort up half of one of the long wobbly lines into a nostril and the other half into the other.

"Wow, this is really pure . . . Can I get a glass of water?"

She nods toward the kitchen and I hand the book back, stand up, and go into the kitchen and get a cold glass of drinking water from the tap and then come back and sit on the floor again. I light a cigarette. The rest of the coke is still on the book.

"You know, Chrissa, this whole thing really makes me feel new. It plays so well to my strengths. A major one of which is you . . ." I'm looking directly into her eyes and she's taking it and looking back. "It's not something one should dwell on too much, but I think we're being . . . molded, like shaped. Not shaped exactly . . . it's hard to explain. The people we are and the circumstances we're in, and Jack and his needs and position and everything, too, are forces that've combined to make this dramatic thing which seems . . . magical, happen. We're creating Jack as much as he's creating us. It's like chemicals or a volcano or something—all the elements take their effect on each other and suddenly there's a new thing in the world, the world is new again. We have it coming and it was meant for us. It was meant to be. Do you know what I mean?"

The coke has numbed the inside of my nose and I can taste it on the back of my tongue, where the whole hollow is going icy. I feel magnificent: invulnerable; fast and clear as a mountain stream.

"Do you think we're new again? Do you think we can get along?"

Argh. She's done it again. I didn't think that was askable. "Well listen, first of all we have to. We're both grown up enough and respect each other enough and want enough for this thing to work, don't we?" My heart is curling up. Then a wave of rush pours through and it swells again. "Chrissa, I'm going to tell you honestly: I love you." *Fuck,* where did that come from? My heart goes crazy for a second, and my throat gets sticky as if I've said something really true and then all of a sudden I feel like one of my fans that I feel sorry for. "I've always loved you." The world has gotten really quiet. "Well maybe I haven't—I know it's what I do that counts, not what I say. But inside myself, it's you that I'm with. Even when I forget it. It doesn't matter what's gone down: Because I met you, because you're with me in a way that no one, not even you, can touch or tamper with or damage, I'm . . . something . . . I don't know what I am. I'm alive, I've been there and it's in me. Maybe it's just a coincidence that it happened with you, this person that I'm sitting here talking to now, or irrelevant, but I'll take it. I don't understand it, I don't know what it means, I know I'm not making any sense, I don't know where any of it leads or anything, but I don't want to be anywhere but in it, doing it. *Shit.*" I can't stand this. I am in bad territory. Her eyes actually look a little wet and I don't even know whether I mean this shit and God knows I sound like an idiot.

I get up and go over and she lets me pull her out of her chair and put my arms around her. She even makes it feel real. It becomes real because of how she accepts it. That must be what makes her amazing and why I do actually love her like nothing else. Don't I? If I knew what that fucking word meant.

"I'm sorry," I whisper, desperately trying to actually know that I'm telling the truth, "I feel like I've cheated or something. I didn't mean to talk like that and mess up your mind or whatever— Can we just lie down for a minute?"

She lets me lead her down to the rug. We lie on the floor pressed together on our sides, with her head in the bend of my arm and her face on my chest. In the silence I have this furious sucking want, which feels like it comes from the dry tear manufactory, where my eyes and throat meet, like a kind of purely internal roaring scream that's constant but I only notice in such rare isolated moments, and I feel like we are together each on the other side of a barrier but it's enough but it isn't enough. I go to kiss her and she kisses me back for an insane second and then stops. She sits up and takes a drink of water from the glass on the floor. She looks tired.

"Billy, not now . . . I can't let you make this trip into a simple dumb love story. Not from now. Maybe I love you, maybe I don't, maybe it doesn't make any difference." She laughs and I do too, because it sounds like a cheap movie. "One thing is that I know you, and I know that you'll take whatever you can. I don't mean that you're not sincere. You just can't help yourself. I wonder if Jack saw all this happening. There's something like the devil of him."

I sit back up against the wall. "Fuck Jack. OK. I can't deny there's a lot to what you say. I almost said it myself a few minutes ago. But I swear it's changing. . . . Maybe not. Maybe I'm just dreaming out of desire. But I'm sick of the way things have been, the way I am . . . I know that's true—"

"Good, and I believe you. And a lot of the way things have been haves been you seducing anyone who could make you like yourself better for a minute or two."

"You *know* that's not what was going on here. Don't take that away from me." I shouldn't have said that. I can't stand the way my voice sounds whiney.

"There's lots of levels to what was going on here, but they're not where our attention should be."

My attention is now on the line of coke still waiting on the table. I can't help feeling like a chastised schoolboy, and that tends to send me into further transgression.

I say, "Could you put that coke away? I don't like it lurking there."

41

We're both surprised.

"OK."

I honestly don't know whether I did that for effect or not. I sip a drink of wine.

"Woo. Quite a ten minutes."

We start talking about the trip. I do have a few ideas. One is to treat it as a detective story, written warped Raymond Chandler–style, about our search for the purpose of the trip. This, I maintain, demands I go incognito and requires a wardrobe budget so that I can dress myself as a normal mid-American. We're laughing and she's caught up in it and advances me $200. A little later I spend five minutes confidently persuading her to take back fifty for half a gram of coke and soon after that I leave.

With money in my pocket and secure knowledge of where and how to trade it for dope I am a cowboy, cold and serene beneath the stars. I pick up another few bags on the way home. The elements are hard but I can deal with them. I am happy with the only happiness that holds: hard knowledge of the terrain.

No one knows but his horse what a cowboy does alone in the desert. This one brightens the furthest hours of the deep dark night in isolated pleasure, shooting coke and then, breathless, taut, intent, and pure, coaxing his dick into its most naked state as he draws it in the mirror. Drawing it out.

When, having concentrated all myself in my groin, I finally achieve apotheosis in voluptuous spurts and gushes of blistering milky slime, I reward myself with a massive dose of junk for sleep and the day is complete.

8

I get my methadone in the morning, but I don't plan to drink it till tomorrow because I still have some dope left.

Methadone is fucked up. The government has it manufactured to give to addicts, so when I first started using it I assumed it was a cure for addiction, that it blocked withdrawal symptoms without creating a habit itself. Then I found out that not only does it get you smeared-out stoned with a heavier hand than junk itself, but that it's also addictive, with an even worse and longer-lasting withdrawal. It's vicious to push it as a solution to addiction. But at least it's cheap.

The government clinics give it away with the ostensible purpose of weaning clients from it as soon as possible. In fact, the clinic staff discourages cutting down. Frustrated, paranoid junkies who really want help to stop figure that they're kept dependent because the program's funding depends on it, but I think it's probably because the doctors in charge know that addiction runs deep; since they aren't supplying real treatment they string along their patients to keep them from going back to street dope. It's all a nasty charade. The program is where old addicts go when they get too tired of the grind. Most of them get high on dope when they can anyway and make a few extra dollars selling surplus milligrams to the needy.

The bitter-tasting stuff comes suspended in astronaut's orange drink in little plastic bottles. You can't shoot it, only drink it. That's why it's so cheap on the street. If I'm careful I can make one $12 bottle last three days. I can get three bottles a week from a neighbor who's on the program with his wife. It's sweet security for the likes of me.

I have no methadone habit at the moment, so my plan is to get three bottles this week, make them last in decreasing doses until we leave, and then hit the road clean. The future looks rosy.

We have three weeks before we fly to California.

I buy myself a thick schoolboy notebook to devote to the trip. Spiral binding, red cardboard cover, lined paper. A blank notebook with a definite purpose is pure creamy power. Its passive fat potential is a self-fulfilling prophesy of potence. I've filled them before; this one has its designation, and, thrillingly, it will be filled as well, with contents that surprise me. If I tend it a little the notebook itself will take care of the trip.

I like the approach of imagining myself as Jack's seedy private eye on a conceptual reverse twist of an assignment to detect the nature of the assignment. It's sort of like *Mr. Arkadin* where Welles, as one of the world's richest and shadiest men, hires a guy to trace his mysterious origins while his secret intention is really to murder everyone the detective turns up because they know too much.

But any of that will come later in the framing of what we gather on the road. Chrissa and I discuss what we'll actually be looking for and decide that it must be sort of rockabilly America, where Jack seems fixed: The America of the fifties, especially in the pockets that are still practically like the nineteenth century electrified. Right before television and franchise merchants homogenized and cheapened it all. That's what Elvis was and why he was so adored. He redeemed the poor and simple, showed the big shots the beauty of a country boy set loose. The way he dressed and moved like a stud-sharp Negro, because he had the same tastes, but always with a disarming little smile that said, Ain't this funny, and he never ever left any room for doubt that first and most of all he loved his mama. Jack Kerouac worked along similar lines, when you could still be an unapologetic poet of the U.S.A. and do it for your mother.

That kind of thing. It's a start anyway, it's a lead.

In another way, the search is as sad and muddled and futile as assassination conspiracy theories, with all the evidence already raked over so endlessly, the mere thought of it is depressing. But I trust my instincts well enough to have faith that I'll find a way to salvage a book's worth. Even if the subject isn't new, we're new, and that will make the book new.

The first order of business is to get me a wardrobe, a style, some camouflage. I want to look like I belong, I want the Americans I want to talk to to want to talk to me. And I am ready for a new identity.

I have a goofy time going around to thrift shops and used-clothing places. The East Village is full of them and most of the clerks know me. I walk in and everybody gets to searching for something American. I get me some pointy-toed shoes, and a bunch of dime-store type sport shirts from the fifties and sixties with big patterns and stripes. I think I'll be safe sticking with my tight black Levi's. I break out the scissors and try to neaten up my hair a little bit, and buy some Dixie Peach pomade to slick it back with. I think I'm remembering back to the seventh grade in Kentucky and then riffing on it. Put me in a '57 DeSoto and I'll light up the map like a pinball machine.

Of course I have Copley to deal with. We have one gig before I go and one rehearsal.

The rehearsal is a disaster. I'm shooting coke that day and it takes everything I have just to force myself to leave the house for the studio. When I get started on coke I don't want to open up a space of even half an hour when I can't get off. The rush is so good and its drop-off so scary. Furthermore, I don't want to go outside because all the sensory input is so amplified that the slightest shift in the environment sets off all my threat responses. I'm out there like a flightless bird, my galvanized face swivelling in little jerky arcs, wild-eyed, as I triple-time for safety.

I bring my works to the rehearsal studio and every thirty or forty minutes I'm walking out of the rehearsal room to go shoot up in the toilet. I am so jittery and wired it takes me forever to find a vein with the needle. Finally I get the shot, half-missing. I run my gory arm under the faucet thinking I have to hurry back to rehearsal to keep the mistrust to a minimum and I stride back all purposeful, heedless that I've left the bathroom splattered red and watery-pink with blood. Then Copley takes a piss himself and when he comes back fuming I can't imagine why he's closed down another five or six excruciating degrees on his contained fury, and I get more resentful behind it myself. It's a circus inside a war zone inside some nasty fucking weather.

The other guys deal with it in their individual ways. The second guitar player has his own problems and operates on the assumption that chaos is built into rock & roll anyway, so he gets along. The drummer is a sleepy guy, fairly new to the band, who just puts in his time without complaining, glad to have a paying job with a popular group. The bass player, Larry, on the other hand, is insufferable. He thinks all the pain and insanity is glamorous. It's fascinating—partly disgusting, partly hilarious—to watch him trying eagerly to fit into this atmosphere of depraved hopelessness.

Copley and I entertain ourselves sometimes by exploiting his determination to belong. I remember one time Copley got him to come over to make a delivery to a girl I'd brought home after a gig. Copley said she'd called for a favor and he asked Larry to take care of it for him. So there's Larry buzzing my door in the middle of the night. He comes upstairs and stalls around, mystifying me, until finally he gets a moment alone with the girl, and, pleased as a proud little puppy, reaches into his magic bag and hands her this huge two-pronged dildo.

Then, when he's made a fool of himself in whatever manner, he acts as if he's really been in on it from the beginning, that he's done it on purpose for our inner-circle benefit, and no amount of amazed disbelief can penetrate his smirk.

He is a marvel. You just can't dent his certainty that all human relations, if not existence itself, are based on pretending that you're pretending. It is just about the saddest thing you can imagine and it makes you want to kill him. Though I scorn and despise him, I kind of puritanically, sado-masochistically, like having him around because of the way he's some kind of caricature illustration of what I stand for. I've made him up in a way, like a male version of Merry: I deserve him; he is some kind of appropriately degrading fun house mirror of me.

The gig goes well enough and largely wins back Copley. I'd

hoped it would work out that way and it does. We open a new club in midtown and the place is packed. We're past our real prime but uptown doesn't know any better, and we also draw all our crowd from the Lower East Side because they're faithful and most of them don't know any better either. Furthermore, we have some new material and are tight on the older stuff from sheer repetition. What clinches it for Copley though is that the sound system, mix, and stage sound are good. This makes it possible for him to play really well, and we've been around long enough that—best of all—they applaud his solos and call out his name. Then, too, if how I am drives him crazy offstage, he appreciates those same qualities in performance. He approves my not giving a fuck when it's directed at the crowd.

Truthfully, the audience bewilders me more than anything else. They have ever since we started drawing anyone outside our original core following. I don't know what they are there for and though I want to give them the benefit of the doubt, all indications confirm the most cynical and demeaning view. They are stupid. They are fools. But, once again, what does that make me? Either a stupid fool myself or a panderer, unless I valiantly try appealing to the best in them, which I'm incapable of doing in any sustained way, or else ignore them and just release everything in the material, showering them with contempt and anger and stunned amazement at the hopeless emptiness of it all, which is what I end up doing. Sometimes it works, sometimes it doesn't; I'm up to it or I'm not. That night it worked, and Copley had his version of a glow, which on Copley is a glower with the *e,r* smudged, something like a junkyard basset that's just caught a rat. I could just see his mind wavering with the recollection that there is a payoff after all, that maybe he's only forgotten about the good part.

It's a nice musical note on which to depart.

9

Today we go.

Chrissa picks me up early in a cab. It's a tremendous spring-drenched early summer morning in New York and I blend with it perfectly. I'm freshly washed, fully packed, newly clothed, and eager for adventure. When I get downstairs, Chrissa's standing by the car smoking a cigarette in the sun. She takes one look at me and starts giggling. I look around, not getting it, and she breaks into a laugh. I grin, trying to join in, mumbling something about my hair, which is pomaded back to my scalp in heavy furrows, but it doesn't help. She's laughing at me. I look at my reflection in a window of the car. My distorted face is very pale and a little puffy with my drug diet and the early hour. The wet hairdo does look a little strange, especially the lesbian-like side-burns, which have nothing to do with facial hair, but are just combings plastered against my jawbone under the sidepieces of my cheap sunglasses. My bone-thin torso is draped in a fifties synthetic shirt that I found at a thrift store. The shirt is white with poker chip-size pinwheels of pink and orange woven in. I figured it'd match our Adventurer. I have on my heavy old brown belt with its big square brass buckle off-center and a length of strap dangling from its cinch down my faithful black jeans. I peer at my lower body. The new orange socks are heavier than the pants and they reach into these slightly scuffed, pointy-toed, old black shoes I bought at a flea market. She keeps saying, "Nothing, nothing," as the driver opens the trunk for us, and we put away our couple of bags for the ride to the airport.

"This is *America*, Chrissa. You wouldn't understand about that," I say as we get in the backseat of the car. That sets her giggling again.

I'm scowling.

"You look . . . you look noble! It's pleasure . . . I laugh with pleasure . . . It's admiration!"

We sit in the backseat as the driver puts the car in gear and pulls away from the building that holds my insane apartment. I turn to Chrissa, grip her above her collarbones, stare her in the eyes significantly, and whisper, "It had to be a comedy, don't you understand?"

"Yes, yes."

"Good. Just remember it's bad form to laugh too hard at our own jokes."

"But of course."

She, naturally, hasn't made any concessions. She wears perfectly creased black-on-black slacks with a subtle raised pattern to the weave, pastel socks, and golden slippers. An overlarge shirt with deep stripes of color is tucked into the pants. She looks great. Like some kind of international love imp.

She'd once told me about having sex with the driver of a cab she'd taken. The husky guy behind the wheel has smiled this canine grin at her as he opened the trunk for us, but I'm pretty sure the dandruff drifting across the dully gleaming shoulders of his cheap suit will have eliminated him. Now filthy Plexiglas removes him farther, so I dismiss him. We drive up First Avenue toward the Midtown Tunnel.

"Isn't it good to be leaving?" I ask. "I've always loved to leave. It makes you feel so *significant* and . . . unknown at the same time. I mean you automatically become a legend in your past, because the real you's not there to ruin it, and then in whatever you're entering you're a mystery, and you can be whatever you want. It's so great."

"You are a little bit crazy."

"What do you mean?"

"Well, it sounds like you want only to be a fantasy."

"Yikes." I think about that for a second. "That's probably bad isn't it? Oh well. I'll take my relief where I can find it."

I watch the streets go by. Already, I feel like reaching over and holding her hand but of course that would be out of line. In the quiet I shift shape in a slow-motion shudder to find myself suffo-cating deliciously in the chill and vacuous cloud of yearning that is produced around me by isolated contact with any half-appeal-ing woman.

I guess she's right: I am just about thirteen, like a wide-eyed cartoon batted back and forth by pop-up semi-emotions that squash me through the world and then I come out the other side to Chinese music, stunned and goofy.

I watch the way I feel, like it's the Macy's parade, bored and amazed. I want out of me and into her.

The airport seems alien. All the self-satisfied people annoy me. I get on the plane in a restless minor anger.

Flying is dead time; it's like going into a closet and waiting for hours until can step out in another location. Of course, the closet is catered, but the caterers treat you like a pod.

I have part of a bottle of methadone in my carry-on bag, but I haven't used any for over a day and I feel a little nuts. As soon as we're airborne I stand and reach up into my bag for the bottle and take it back to the bathroom where I drink a little. The instant I taste the bitter powdery juice my mood improves.

There is plenty of room on the plane so when I pull out my notebook, Chrissa graciously moves a few seats away. I'm enter-ing my new identity as reporter. I sit with my notebook on my lap, waiting for the drug to warm me. I haven't eaten yet so I know it will come on soon.

The brutish matrons are slowly careening up the aisle behind me with their cart of fake hospitality. I can remember when the sluts were warm. Once I passed sixteen their hostility rose through. They could sense I'd opted out.

A rum and Coke will do and I damn well want the whole can.

I have my domain here. It's only three seats wide, but what the hell. I am the Observer and it all belongs to me. I smile at myself, retract my reach, my field, and then, looking out the win-dow, project it out across the clouds.

I write in my notebook, "Nature is so tolerant." It's comfort-ing and austere and final, the way one's author should be. Curse it and curse it and it holds its peace; you just get your echo. Whatever you do, you do to yourself. Clouds used to drive me crazy, the way they didn't notice me. Now I can relish the secret knowledge that we are family, that the stuff was always there to take me in, and that that is where the future really leads. I love that feeling of emptiness, of just being a mirror for the clouds. I drift. Why did mind, why did life have to enter? The fact is that we are mud, but we are mud that speaks: talking mud. In the beginning was the Word and there is no way out. Too far in to go backward, and all that is left is language and "death."

Unfortunately, all this chatter isn't going to contribute much to the book, I'm afraid. The drug is coming on, seeping through my system from my stomach, calming me and creating a cushion against all nastiness. A rising push of impulse lifts me out of my seat and I move over beside Chrissa, where she's sitting with a drink, and take the back of her neck in my hands and kiss her on the eyelids. She actually blushes.

"What are you doing?" she asks.

"Scuse me while I kiss the sky."

"I'm not a guy."

"No, you're the sky."

"I'm the sky?"

"Yeah."

"The sky's the limit."

"You're the limit."

"That's what I said," she says.

Ha. I tell her I've been communing with the clouds and I've gotten kind of sleepy. I lower my seatback, close my eyes around a nice little lost-lamb-in-the-woods feeling I've located, and let my temple rest against her hair and shoulder to nod for a few thousand miles.

10

I've only been to Los Angeles two or three times before, passing through with the band. It's nothing like a city. In New York you're in it, in Los Angeles you're on it, like a board marker. It's a surface—a thin-spread, cracked, pastel layer painted on a dry resistant ground. Everywhere there are false signals of cheer. The conspicuous electric signs and elaborate architecture are like smiles pasted onto fear. And then there's the frightening sweet smell of the place, like an orchid's ulterior motive, disgustingly attractive, like the smell of your own farts.

But I'm glad to be here. It's great to be anywhere as a writer. It saves you from implication in the ugliness of a place and justifies your being there. You can spend all day jerking off as long as you describe it well.

We take a cab to our motel, Bessie's Sunset, along wide empty boulevards crisscrossed with electric wires and cables, through tall rows and squat eruptions of foreign palm, low buildings, and broad intimations of the unseen ocean that couldn't care less.

The cab pulls off an anonymous strip of car lots and convenience stores onto the gravel that leads to Bessie's office and leaves us there. The Sunset is painted that California pale pink-orange color that also suggests the husks of small mollusks and mammal interiors or what lurks inside skimpy bathing clothes.

Which brings me to Jennifer, the girl behind the desk. She looks like someone I might have seen in a hardcore porn magazine. I'm instantly comfortable with her. Her character is in her breasts and her perky voice. In fact, they're similar: large, unguarded, and high-pitched, as squeaky as two balloons rubbed together. She's the kind of woman who seems innocent and unshockable at the same time. The overgrownchildlike stuff of fifties sex appeal and California cliché.

I hit it off with her right away, but Chrissa is distant and condescending. I can't help playing on the situation. When Jennifer, cocking her friendly eyebrows a little, teasing, says she has the twin bed room we've reserved, I nod toward Chrissa to explain, "She snores." This is a bad mistake.

We walk past the swimming pool to our room.

Inside Chrissa is really angry. It makes her French accent pop through. "Do you like zat kind of girl?"

"No, I prefer you."

"You lie—you speak to her at my cost."

"I was only joking," I whine.

"You can't make it somesing else by just saying! You insulted me!"

Helplessly, I grin. "Lots of people snore. It's not so—"

"No! I do not snore! Because you made me small to be close to her!"

"I'm sorry, I really am. . . . When you snore I hear symphonies."

"Zat's not funny! I do not snore! And anyway it's not the point! Who do you sink you are?! Zis is impossible." She has her suitcase open on the bed and is exchanging the sweater she's wearing for something lighter. She stomps toward the door.

"I am. I am sorry," I say, moving to intercept her. She won't allow it. I can't get the goddamn smile off my face but I'm embarrassed and feel like a jerk. A reasonable question strikes me and I ask, "Where are you going?"

"I'm going out! I'm going for a walk."

"There's nowhere to walk in L.A."

"Maybe I'll call a cab," she says. She takes her camera with her as she stomps out the door. She pushes it hard and it closes between us.

I don't go after her, but her ominous last line swells in my head, and I am paying. I go and sit on the bed and look at the floor.

I am badly miscast as a hero, even of my own book.

I wish I had a joint.

I get up and go over and pull open the curtain on the window that's beyond the beds.

The view, my solitude, and the softening effects of the methadone in my system are asserting their power of oblivious equilibrium.

Out back is a fenced patch of motel property and then the yard to a low little stucco house. The sun is bright and behind the motel the abrupt emergings and returns of birds and butterflies among the chaos of shrubbery look gorgeous and amazing, like transubstantiation. The foliage is boiling with life. Across the lot, a woman emerges from the back door of the house with a large basket in her arms. She is pretty, but her clothes look faded and poor, and she seems forlorn to me. There's wash hanging on a line, but first she puts the basket down and starts gathering some of the toys that are littering her yard. My heart gets pulled open. I love her. It's a lot easier to love someone from a distance, I think, banally. I want a joint.

Jennifer comes to mind. I wonder if I can see her without Chrissa knowing, and whether Jennifer will allow it. The idea of walking over there and speaking to her gives me a lift. Then a sudden intimation of myself as a white rat, or a little child left alone, drawn toward the reward and shrinking from the punishment. What the hell. I just want a joint; I'm sick of being myself and thinking and everything.

I go in the bathroom and wash up a little.

I pull open the door to the motel courtyard like the Lone Ranger, facing new vistas.

The office is empty, but there is a doorway behind the desk and in a moment Jennifer comes through it. "You're not really Billy Bernhardt," she says, "you're Billy Mud."

"And who are *you* really?"

"I'm me," she says, unimpressed with my repartee, but uncritical I think.

"I have a little problem I thought you might be able to help me with. I'd really like to have some smoke. Might you be able to help me with that?"

"You want some weed?"

"Yeah."

"I've got some right back here. You want to smoke some?" She's barefoot and wearing a short batik muumuu.

"Yeah . . ."

"Come on," she says, starting back toward the room.

I duck under the counter and follow her, saying, "I'd like to buy some to have some for later."

"Well, see if you like it."

"OK."

The room behind the office is like a suburban den, with a big soft couch pushed off from the back wall and a couple of armchairs out across from it. A low coffee table piled with old magazines sits in front of the couch. There are half-closed drapes on the large window to the street. She closes the door behind us and goes and pulls a gauzy underlayer of curtains together beneath the drapes. My throat tightens a little bit in anticipation of being isolated with her as I wait by the couch. She comes back and we sit down side by side.

She reaches for an already rolled joint among the things on the coffee table and lights it.

"What are you doing here?" she asks. "Is that your girlfriend?"

Within three sentences, the game is on: The object of the conversation is to keep her thinking I'm worth having sex with without letting on that it makes any difference to me at all. The second part's not too hard—it's gotten to where the hassles of contact are almost more than they're worth. It is just about as appealing to me to file her in my imagination and jerk off later.

Then again, I'm already getting that lassitude of syrupy blood that has me wanting to swamp and liquefy across her mouth and eyes and hair and tits and hips and legs and feet until she learns to breathe it or suck and drink herself to land. I'm getting a hard-on, and when she gets up and goes to the windows to pull the heavy drapes closed I take it as a signal that private, personal, activity is now due to commence. I rub between my legs as her back is to me, just to make sure, and then reach in my pants and flip my impending hard-on up my belly the length of my fly so it has more room to grow.

She turns from the window with an easy smile and is walking back toward me in the dim room. I stand up and say, "Hey—wait a minute—turn around." I walk over and flick gently above her shoulder blades. It's amazing the heartspinning electrical power, dropping my jaw and giving me x's for eyes, that just that little touch in the dim quiet produces. Then I rub there with two fingers as she says, "What is it?" "Well . . ." I explain, and put the flat of my hand there, sliding it gently around and the other hand to her abdomen and pulling the back of her against me. I know she can feel my vertical hard-on squashed in the crack of her butt. "Billy, what—" she starts to ask, but I'm turning her around. The squishy resilience of her big breasts against my chest is like perfect homecoming. She doesn't stop me from kissing her and then she's kissing back.

Apart from the loose scrap of dress, she has nothing on but panties. In a moment both are on the floor and I bend her over the couch and fuck her from behind.

It's like a dream. You're a child born of lust and you trust it. They are all as little children. The energy streams off as my eyes go glazey and I am a zombie for it, a floppy pencil in mama nature's hand, writing lucky numbers and drawing naked women as I lengthen and harden and the stakes get raised until the bank breaks and all the haze goes golden. But there's nothing to trade it for and its value plummets. Where did all that money go? I guess God took it. It's fun though, as they say in California.

As we part in a wet and smelly heap on the couch a sumptuous few seconds afterward, I start to sense her presence again and my cock stirs. I kiss her. She moves down and stoves her mouth around the head of my dick, but I want to stretch it out and keep her admiration, so I push her up onto the seat and slide to the floor, my eyes before her hairy crotch. I feel the flicker of her passing self-consciousness. My scratchy chin scrapes against the back of my hand as I plunge into the froth, hand and mouth. Her vagina inflates till it feels like a ribbed balloon inside and I can hardly find its edges. I know she's near to coming. She's sighing in howls. The balloon pops into spasms and she convulses around it, wailing. I straighten on my knees, slide the endlessly reaching, groping stiffness from my groin up into her and in no time at all it releases its floody urge to search way on up her rainy alleyways for another few hours as I slip away like a ghost.

For a second I think it's in my head, but it's too harsh: The bell in the office has rung. I'm sure who it is. She's stepped from the back of my mind into the front of the building.

I look at Jennifer. Strands of wet hair are stuck to the edges of her face, her color is high, and her eyes are elsewhere, but the sound of the bell is bringing her back. She smiles unaffectedly. "I'm coming," she says. I jump up, grab my clothes, and balance against the wall behind where the door would open, pulling on my underwear. It's hateful to break that good sleepy feeling and I try to keep some of it. Jennifer calls out, "Coming," as she grins and stumbles off the couch gathering up her two pieces of clothing. She steps into a little closet of a bathroom, half shuts the door, and turns on the sink. "Be right there!"

Oh fuck. Well, it's perfect. A drama's been created and I won't have to figure out how to treat her now. I absolutely know who is outside.

When Jennifer comes out I whisper that if that's Chrissa, don't give her any idea it's me in the back room. She looks stoned and she wants to talk it over but there isn't any time. I listen at the door as she goes to the desk.

"Hi," says Chrissa. Half-stoned, my brain has this logical paranoid insight that if I know it's her, she knows it's me.

"Hi."

"I went out without the key. Do you have it?"

"Why would I have it?" Jennifer returns suavely.

"Because my friend's not in the room. I'm hoping he left it here."

"Oh. No, he didn't."

"Well, I guess I'll just wait here a little while. Until he comes back."

"You don't have to do that because we have a spare."

"Good. You have seen him at all?"

Chrissa. I know what she's doing and I feel guilty as shit all the way through the door. She's staring into Jennifer's eyes for a reaction and it's obvious Jennifer isn't a good liar.

"Who? Billy? No."

"Well, thanks." Chrissa walks out.

As Jennifer comes back through the door I have my finger to my lips. Maybe Chrissa will walk right back in to overhear something. My adrenalin is a little sexy, but mostly I feel stranded and the first lapping wavelets of self-hatred. Oh no. Here I am again alone with myself.

I grab Jennifer and half-swallow her tongue for dear life. I want to lick her crotch again.

No. I have to think. I tell her to look and make sure Chrissa is actually returning to the room. She half-resentfully goes to a little window in the bathroom and says, "Yeah."

I say, "Jesus, you look sexy . . . I've gotta think. I'm really sorry about this, but me and Chrissa have a long history and we've gotta do a lotta traveling together and I don't wanna make it weird from the beginning. Understand?"

"Whatever," she says, pulling off her muumuu again.

"No, no," I insist, and her nipples in my mouth are as big and hard as ballpark bubblegum, like giant pencil erasers.

"I can't do this. I can't do this. Put this back on." I pick up the dress and turn away and swing it behind me to her. She does look sexy, but Chrissa's on my mind, plus I feel like I might just be going on biological reflex and, on top of everything else, I don't want to find out my dick is too numb to keep up.

She presses herself against me from the back, her hands cupping my crotch. I pull away, saying, "I mean it Chrissa—I mean—? . . . Jennifer—"

That does it. She puts the dress on and she acts angry.

I get her to give me a couple of joints anyway, and say I hope to see her later, and I sneak out the front door and across the street.

So this is America. I'm sitting among the Dumpsters on a curb in back of a convenience store holding a cardboard container of coffee trying to compose myself for a convincing performance for Chrissa. It's a pretty day and the coffee is good, but I should get back to the motel room soon, before she can think too much. "Fuck shit piss," I say to myself.

Fuck shit piss: another mantra. I remember catching myself in New York silently repeating those words in my head.

I don't feel as if I've exactly done anything wrong. I am myself and there it is, but I'm going to lie to Chrissa. I feel squeezed by circumstances, I feel wronged and innocent. But I can't consider telling the truth any more than I'd think about reaching into a fire to see how hot it is. I just have to seal off my mind from the possibility. But I keep wanting to think it could be possible to tell her the truth. I don't know which is more selfish. I guess it was a mistake to sleep with Jennifer. "Sleep." Maybe it *was* sleep, maybe that's the problem. Maybe I'm sleepwalking and I need to wake up. But shit, I'm just a man. I can't be perfect and we're built that way.

Sitting on the sunny curb I feel like a hole in the landscape, like a cigarette burn. My edges are smoldering and my center is empty. I put down the coffee, stand up, and start walking in circles around the whirring nothing, the shifting force walls, of my brain. I'm like a satellite building up speed to break orbit from the sucking void and angle off into space. In a moment I veer off in the direction of the room.

As I convey myself past the back corner of the store, across oil-stained concrete, through molecules of odor, the sunlight on my face, cars noisily crossing larger and smaller ahead, I consolidate, returning toward the target and who I have to be there.

By the time I arrive I'm solid, I'm physical. I put the key in the lock, push the door open, and go inside.

Chrissa is on the floor covered in blood.

Just kidding. She's lying on her bed reading a book.

"Hi," she says.

"Hi."

"Where'd you go? You took the key."

"Oh. I'm sorry. I walked around, had a cup of coffee."

"Me, too. I took some pictures."

"I'm sorry about how I acted earlier Chrissa."

"Watch it."

"What?"

"Never mind," she says a little sharply.

"I think I'm going to take a shower."

"OK."

I slide off my shoes, reach into my suitcase for clean socks and underwear, and go into the bathroom.

Maybe things are a little better, maybe they'll be all right. Maybe she doesn't really want to know and this will blow over.

I lock the bathroom door, get undressed, and get into the shower. Just as I grab the soap there's a knock on the bathroom door.

"Billy, I have to get something out of there."

"All right." I stretch out on one leg to unlock the door and then jump back into the tub. As I stand in the spray behind the curtain I feel vulnerable that she's out there pissed off and fully dressed, but I'm also a little excited that she's chosen to come into the bathroom while I'm naked in here. Who knows, maybe she's naked too. I try to interpret her fuzzy shadow on the shower curtain and listen to her movements through the blankets of water while continuing to soap myself as if everything is normal. I am really tense but getting more turned on.

All of a sudden there's a terrific crash and I'm exposed in the overhead light and the two little rooms, one wet and one dry, become one and this thing unbends, letting go of the shower curtain that it's just half ripped from the bent rod and stands facing me full on. Her face looks squashed and red and green as if she's wearing war paint. She has her puffy hand to her face and I realize my dirty underwear is in it. She's smelled it. I am paralyzed. She throws the underwear at me. She bends and picks up all the rest of my clothes, clean and dirty, and heaves them at me. I still haven't moved but I feel peculiarly empowered as her assault accelerates and she starts to yell. She screams, "You bastard, you had sex with that bitch! You lying shit! You know what you are! You're shit!" Then she starts picking up heavier ammunition—a can of shaving cream, a jar—and throwing them as hard as she can at me. I reach and almost fall out of the tub, grabbing for the front of her shirt. I pull the blouse so hard it rips and she bangs her shins on the edge of the tub, and as I'm yanking and half-lifting her across into the cone of shooting water she hits me in the temple with a fist of perfume bottle and I see stars for an instant. I'm struggling to hold her and not fall and by then she's crying. There's blood on her hand. I get hold of the back of her neck and pull her face to mine and our teeth knock against each other. The kiss is like a movie within a movie: another mindless, violent, unstoppable gush of impulse that is going on just below the surface of the earth as the explosions continue above. We kiss so hard it isn't even us, it's our parents or their parents or our children or something trying to get somewhere, spirits released via our heads and we drink each other's chewy teeth against teeth and suck and mangle our tongues as if they are everything and we want to live, our crotches, but harder and harder. I'm almost crying too, but am dry inside away from my mouth and our faces are pressed against each other until the bones will break kissing people who aren't even us or anybody as hard as we can as if it would do any good. And this of course is like a movie too, but nature has done it, somehow the segue has been inevitable you realize with a crushing exhilarated clarity . . . When I draw back and see her eyes, she is out of them, they have no meaning but some ongoing rush. Her shirt is torn open and I grab the front of her flimsy bra where it clasps and twist and yank and it gives. I look at the breasts I haven't seen for so long, and in that moment she hits me in the face as hard as she can and I fall down in the soaked muck of my clothes. She steps out of the tub, incredibly gorgeous, turns to look at me and says, "Maybe some other time."

12

Things go smoothly enough the rest of the night. We have some Chinese food delivered and call the mechanic who is tuning up the car. We'll be able to pick it up in the morning. I write in my notebook and Chrissa takes some pictures. Our contact is more tense and delicate but it's more personal.

At bedtime we smoke a joint—I don't tell her where it came from—and we are laughing. Too giddy, I ask, "Is it another time yet," but, happily, she pretty much lets me get away with it, saying that with me it's always 3:00 fucking A.M. I'm not so dumb as to press the point, but even stoned it's difficult to fall asleep with her in the next bed.

I lie in bed conscious of her presence a few feet away in the dark and it moves me. I just admire her; I think I could worship her for the level of spiritual competence she inhabits beyond me. At the same time I'm exalted by the seriousness with which she takes me. I'm thankful to her, and for once it is even apart from any desire, sexual or otherwise. I am just glad she walks the world.

I want to give her something. I go and get a towel from the bathroom and hang it over the bedside lamp and I pull out my notebook and a pencil and get back under the covers and start writing. I close my eyes and think of her. I want to tell her about the secret plane upon which we crawl in and out of each other while the flight attendants clap and take off their clothes. And the colors, the colors . . . someone is whispering on his deathbed. Is it Orson Welles or Marlon Brando? Horror rosebud, protect us from wrong turns and let the ones we love . . .

Oh, well, I've never been able to write on command. Instead, I finish writing about everything that's happened today.

The next day the morning is beautiful.

We take a taxi to get the car. We are both excited.

The car is being held by a guy in Venice named Bob. He has a beard and a beer belly and the DeSoto is in front of his garage. The house is a ramshackle, junk-filled shack. The guy is obviously a bachelor, and, predictably, he likes talking to Chrissa. I hate these situations. Every guy who ever sees her wants her attention and I'm nothing but petty interference. But she never embarrasses me by encouraging it, except maybe if she's drunk and pissed off at me and the guy seems interesting.

The car is a dream come true. A time machine. It has an aura. It is the color of fire—the color of New York methadone—and when you look at it everything else goes away. Inside it we feel like we have a domain. It's hard to believe that it's only machinery, just material. Parked there in the seedy overgrown lots of Venice, it seems like a secret hiding in plain sight, like the purloined letter.

The car is low to the ground with a wide bulging face, the bottom two-thirds of which are coated in long curves of streamlined, heavy chrome. On either side above, squinting from the pale orange, are pairs of headlights nestled in sculpted rings of more chrome. The lights tip rolls of fender that don't end for eighteen feet, where on either side of the car they sweep up into chrome and triple taillight fins sharper and higher than I've ever seen on a car before. The black roof floats on a swell of glass that's like an elegant blister on this massive orange wedge. The color is fire, but the finish on the paint job isn't glossy anymore, and it looks dim and hidden, like a fire in the sunlight.

We want to get it on the road, so we sign some papers for Bob, collect some more, and get directions to Highway 1. We figure we'll take the road along the coast up to San Francisco before heading east. I don't think it out—I just allow myself to semi-consciously take it for granted—but a lot of the reason I want to go there is because I have hardly any methadone left and I know I can find drugs in San Francisco.

Inside the car, both seats are like couches, and the gearshift is a cluster of five little push buttons on the dash to the left of the gigantic but spare steering wheel. The speedometer seems to stretch across half the dashboard and below it are two long rows of knobs and gauges. There's a working watch imbedded in the hub of the steering wheel. The car feels like a home and it feels like an idea—a fast, spectacularly decorated room that you can pilot.

We head up the coast past the wide, congested roads of L.A. onto the classic two-lane that rises and dips and winds its way among the cliffs and forests at the edge of the sea all the way to San Francisco.

Really, neither of us have ever known anything like it. I've never owned a car. I've been a stranger and a vagrant often enough, but never with these secret powers of self-renewing pocket money and a fire-colored car. Not to mention a dream woman who likes me. And on top of everything we are all real. The car may weigh close to two tons but right away it's at 95 mph and there's plenty left. Imagination is one thing, but this is really interesting. You could get hurt. Being behind the wheel is an adventure in itself. In these fifties cars they wanted it to seem effortless, but thirty years later you really feel connected to the works. It's mechanical, not electronic: your mind is making the decisions and your muscles are extensions of the car's mechanisms. The personality of the car is not only in the way it looks, but in the quirks and leanings and urges you feel with your hands and feet and arms and legs as you respond to each other while getting somewhere. It's something you want to do as well as you possibly can and it matters. These cars are crazy of course—we'll be getting ten or twelve miles a gallon, and a crash would be gruesome what with all the sharp edges and no seat belts, but you are there in it, tending the engine, not removed or restrained by layers of restrictive choices made for you in advance. You feel as if your destiny is available and you can comprehend and bend it with a little work and practice. Then when it's going smoothly, you can dream, and there is a rhythm. You deal with curves and obstacles like a juggler or a cowboy, not losing the beat, as you carry on your conversation or reveries within the vista. Taking the curves along the cliffs overlooking the ocean, I fall into a smooth state of ecstasy.

Highway 1 is spectacular but it does feel a little self-conscious.

Driving through the fringes of the redwood forests, you feel as if you've been invited into a rich person's house. Maybe you've even been left there alone, but you know that if you make a funny move chances are the alarms will sound and grim men with shoulder holsters will leap from the woodwork. It looks quiet and virginal but it's all national parks and tycoons' estates. The traveler's accommodations aren't motels anymore but lodges, and they have chefs.

We push through it and get nearly to San Francisco before we decide to stop for the night.

13

The next morning I spot a car wash across from the joint where we're getting breakfast. As soon as we order, I go out and take the car over there and as I'm paying the kid in charge he asks me, "What country are you from?"

"What? What *country* am I from? I'm from the U.S.A."

"Oh, you are?"

"Yes."

"Oh."

The joke is on me. As I walk back across the street to the diner I laugh once out loud. I feel a little giddy and weird. When I sit in the booth and tell Chrissa about it my eyes water at the strangeness. Who the fuck am I? How could that have happened? Obviously, she's been right about the way I've gotten myself up, the wardrobe, but I still can't understand what he was reacting to. I don't mind, I've considered myself a stranger for a long time, but how could I have been so wrong?

Chrissa, beauty that she is, doesn't rub it in.

We get to San Francisco before noon and find a motel right away in a seedy district right across the bridge. All that's on my mind, really, is drugs. I have a good idea who to call because I've had a few adventures here stopping over with the band. There is this all-girl group called the Jungle Urban Girls I've hung out with. They're speed freaks. I put in a call to Kathy Jungle Girl as soon as we get to our room. She isn't there and I leave a message. Chrissa and I decide to take the car into town and look around. Driving is a mistake—I'm not maneuvering the car well enough yet—and parking is impossible, but we finally find a space.

The placid, civilized, beauty of the city is irritating me. I want a drink right away. I pull Chrissa into a dark bar with me and order a couple of rounds.

There are two guys at tables writing in notebooks. I've seen this in the espresso shops but apparently they're everywhere. All the people in this town think they're writers. I wonder what the fuck they're writing about. With the help of a bottle of beer, I drink a double scotch in about three minutes and order another single. I'm scattering sparks of restless jittery temper, chafing at the atmosphere, making Chrissa laugh. I say, "Come on," deciding to go and talk to this guy sitting in the middle of the room at a little round table filling his notebook.

"May we join you for a minute?"

He looks up, a long, bony blond guy in wire-rim glasses. He has an open look on his face.

"Sure."

We sit down. "I was wondering what you were writing about and why."

"I'm writing in my diaries. Why? I don't know."

"Why are you doing it here?"

He thinks for a second. "To pick up boys."

"Oh." I turn to Chrissa and say, "We've got a live one," turn back, and ask, "How about couples?" Chrissa kicks me under the table.

"Sorry, I don't like women that way."

"I know what you mean. They are kind of disgusting, aren't they? All soft and everything, and they just envelop you, like the Blob, and they're never satisfied."

"Why don't you shut up?"

"Man. Wow. I'm sorry. I just got caught up in it. I'm really interested in you."

"Who the hell are you?"

"We're agents of destruction. Agents of inquiry."

"That's interesting. Who appointed you?"

"You know, I've been wondering about that myself. The earliest thing I can remember is a kind of burning cloud. There was running chrome, like mercury. It all got thinner and cooled. Then it seemed to be behind us and we were inside something.

We were speeding down the highway in a big orange car, and this is where it's taken us."

"Sounds like the fairies have got you."

"Maybe that's it. Would you read me what you've been writing?"

He hesitates a minute and then looks down at the page. " 'A big skinny dumb-looking tourist at the bar keeps staring at me. Not my type. Uh oh, here he comes.' "

Still, I plow on. "What is your type?"

"I like them young and innocent."

"I can do that," I said.

"Too late."

The fucker is beating me at my own game.

Chrissa interrupts, "Hi, my name is Chrissa. What's yours?"

"Steve."

"I apologize for my friend here."

"I think your friend can speak for himself."

"Not as well as I thought," I say.

"Don't sulk, now," he says.

"I'm all right. Are you really trying to pick up boys?"

"Yeah."

"I don't see how it can work. It seems like everybody in this town is writing in a notebook."

"Well, it's not original, but up until today it usually attracted the kind of guys I wanna attract. Not that you're all that awful."

I look at Chrissa, kind of amazed at this conversation. "You want the kind of shy, sensitive ones . . ."

"Right. They come here from Nebraska to behave like themselves which, believe me, isn't behaving."

"What do you do for a living?"

"I work eve shift at a phone answering service. Why are you asking me all this?"

"I'm a writer too—she's a photographer. We're on assignment. Listen, is there any chance we could get you to show us around a little bit? Like to take us out? We'd pay for everything."

"What's your 'assignment'?"

"A book about America."

"Hm. That narrows it down. Take you out where?"

"Like to gay places. The craziest gay places."

"I don't think so. Anyway, she couldn't get in."

"Why not? She could be a dyke. Or a boy."

Chrissa said, "I can be a boy."

"That would be kind of fun, but these guys aren't there to be gawked at by tourists."

"Of course not, I know that, but I can behave. I'm not really a . . . homophobe or whatever. I'd probably have sex with men myself if I had more balls. Maybe I will. Chrissa has sex with women. We're not out to judge; we just wonder what it's like here. And we'll pay for everything. We'll take you to a really good dinner."

"Maybe. I don't know. I think I'd feel like a traitor taking a couple of straight people in there, especially writers. I'll have to think about it."

"We're only going to be here for two or three days. Could I have your phone number?" I take out a pen and my little pocket notebook pad. "We're staying at this motel."

I copy down the name and numbers. He looks at them.

"Does this say 'Mud'? You're Billy Mud? I've heard of you."

"Yeah. I'm a musician. But I got hired to do this book."

"Well, I work from four o'clock to twelve o'clock. Maybe we could meet after work. You can call me there anyway, if you keep it short. Here's home and work. I'll think about it."

"Great." I stand up and drink the last drops of whiskey. Chrissa stands up too. "We've gotta be going," I say.

Chrissa says, "It was very nice to meet you."

"Yeah, you too. Be good."

Chrissa and I walk out of the bar.

I'm happy for a few minutes. I put my arm around Chrissa's shoulder and say, "Wow, we're really started now." We float down the street, laughing about what'd happened in the bar, but there's a weird taste to everything.

We're walking around, window shopping and looking at it all when I see the strangest thing across the street. It's a pale and beautiful young girl with long wavy red hair who has a boa constrictor wrapped around her upper body. The strange thing is that the snake is exactly the same color as she is. It has pale red-orange markings on cream-colored skin. It looks like an hallucination. No one else seems to notice her particularly. Chrissa doesn't see her and I don't point her out.

Before long we find an excellent used bookstore and spend an hour inside, longer than Chrissa wants to. When we get to our parking space, the car isn't there. It's been towed for being illegally parked.

We make a couple of phone calls and go down to the auto pound and stand in line and pay money and finally get it back. The cop in the cage asks me what country I'm from.

——— 14 ———

Back in the motel room, Chrissa asks, "You'd like to make love with men?"

I'm still fucked up from those drinks. Feeling worn out.

"Well, when I've had enough coke and there weren't any girls around I've thought about it . . . I get so into my own cock, I don't know why I couldn't get into someone else's. It's just sex. . . . But then the problem is who would you do it with? It's too messy when they're human. Has all these unappealing repercussions and subtexts. Couldn't see myself in that situation."

"And what was it you sayed about women—they're a blob?"

Shit. "I was just teasing the guy. Give me a break, Chrissa. I'm really tired and fucked up."

"OK."

"I need to take a nap."

There's a phone message from Kathy waiting. She says she'll be done rehearsing at 7:00 tonight and we should get together.

I'm grouchy in my drunken San Francisco nobodiness. I still have just enough lingering methadone relief that with the sedative of the alcohol I ought to be able to sleep. My eyelids weigh five pounds and my head ninety. I figure that by the time I come to, Kathy ought to have some drugs for me.

There's nothing for a dirty soul like clean tight sheets. Jesus, I love motels.

When I wake up I'm alone and it's half dark out. It's depressing to wake up as it's getting dark. I feel like a dirty act of chance in the dead room. My mouth is dry and tacky and my muscles feel polluted.

I turn on the bedside lamp and see a note from Chrissa by the telephone between the beds. She's gone out with her camera. I pull myself up through dense layers of stupidity to sit on the edge of the bed. Here I am back here amid this hurt and fear. My base state, the one that always underlies everything, no matter how well I can cover it temporarily with distracting activity. A shred of nightmare dream blowing by gets caught on a thorn in my brain, but I can't guess its context or even hold onto it. It's just a sudden black gasp from below that's made a passing lunge for my heart. When I reach, it disintegrates like a flake of ash on my fingertips. I taste them and they taste of wasted life, failure, and hopelessness. There is no one to tell this to. Who could care? I wouldn't. Only the page. I pick up my notebook and write for a couple of minutes.

I go into the bathroom and wash my face and brush my teeth and then come back and call Kathy. She's glad to hear from me and she says she has what I need. I tell her I'll be over in a few minutes. I call a cab.

In the cab I'm thinking about the trip, wondering what I'm doing. It's like a giant hand is pushing me around. It's all I can do to catch the quickest sliding glimpse of the outside world through the fist. There's something appealing in being an outlaw, moved by different forces than the straight world, but it's too confining too. I don't want to be defined by any relationship to social groups, much less by artificial physical cravings. I want to be free.

It starts to rain a little.

Kathy lives in the basement where her band rehearses. The whole basement is bent wire. She collects wire and makes indecipherable shapes out of it. There's wire stapled and soldered to the guitars and amps, wire hanging from the ceiling, jammed into the walls, and accumulating on every available surface. The harsh overhead lighting adds to the effect. The room feels like meaningless cruelty.

I like Kathy though and she likes me, the way only another drug user can. She understands me. She has that good maternal instinct of my favorite women drug dealers. She wants to take care of me like a big spider.

When I'm with her, drugs are the only language. She keeps her TV on all the time and one of her favorite pastimes is speculating about what drugs the parade of TV personalities is using. She'll go, "See! He can't hold his head still. He's trying to decide whether to get up and do a cartwheel or to run right out of that studio as fast as he can out into the parking lot. It's coke. Johnny won't have him back soon." Or, "Barbiturates. No question. You can tell from her hair."

The moment I walk in it's like I've never been anywhere else.

She's tall and her long black hair is as tangled as her sculptures. She wears scraps of distressed black leather and thrift-shop pickings. Her complexion—white with masses of makeup base—is bad, not because she has acne but because she has to scratch and worry any little eruption until it bleeds.

I actually had sex with her once. I'm glad I did it—once is always good for purposes of mutual confidence—but I'd have to be extremely stoned for it to ever happen again. She smells strong—there's body odor, but worse is all the perfume on top of it, and her cunt is floppy below the hard pubic bone and it reeks of piss and fungus. Her big breasts are like mush and there are two or three long wiry hairs protruding from the flat brown nipples. It's like her nervous system is too busy and her sexual parts have gone flaccid. She still wanted sex, but the drive had sped way ahead of her body. It was like having sex with a cloud of static electricity. Every time I see her now, the sensation of those afterthought breasts with their huge 2-D nipples, like haired birthmarks, underlies her presence to me.

She likes to please me though and she has the drugs. It's good to see her.

I shoot a little speedball of a bag of dope mixed with a couple of lines of crystal meth. The rush is sweet. It shakes me—I ripple to my tailbone and shoot to the top of the world. I start to tell her about the trip I'm on and everything I've thought along the way.

She listens to me with little grins of proud indulgent affection and many solemn nods of agreement as she wanders intently around the basement tending to her wire lair. I tell her about the guy in the bar this morning. I tell her about driving the car. I tell her about her wire sculptures and about how well they represent the way everything is interlinked. I tell her about birds and butterflies blending into shrubbery between me and a stranger I'd never see again but whom I'm describing now. I tell her about how nothing is better than drugs.

I lead her outside to stand in the cool light rain for a moment and then I have to do it again because it's so transcendentally delicious it triggers cascading internal shudders of the impossibility of my nerves processing the quantities of pleasure, the excess seeming to drain and eddy into my cock, which gains a delightful ponderous tingling weight.

Sure enough, she starts seeming sexually attractive and I know it's time to go, even though three hours have passed and I've hardly begun. I'm tempted to think up something really dirty to do with her, but she'll always be here later, and I want to get back to the motel and Chrissa. Someone else should have the benefit of my insights. I take a healthy packet of the speed and a set of works and the rest of the bags of dope Kathy's gotten me.

She gives me an umbrella as I step back outside, but I don't use it. I walk in the sprinkling rain like a lion. Pretty soon there won't be lions anymore. If I have to die to be a lion I'll die. I'm roaring, but in the language of rain and sand: I am invisible, I blend in, and I'm not hungry so everyone is safe. I can just observe them, join them, I can admire them, I can pity them and love them. They're so pathetically beautiful I could cry. How could I ever forget that the world is this gorgeous and interesting? Every little detail is a gateway to huge canyons of knowledge and understanding. And it's all so sexy. Nothing is restrained, everything is perfectly, ripely, ravishingly itself, and swollen with signs and information that link it in the web.

The streets glisten and glitter. Occasionally I feel conspicuous for a moment and paranoiac fear engulfs me, but I know it's irrational and I shake it off. After a few blocks, I realize I'm lost but since everything ends up where it begins I'm not terribly worried. I feel too large for the streets though. The other minds out here, each with its own super-complex formation of aims and motives, are threatening and take too much effort to track. It's amazing how much you can tell in a glance—how much psychology is present in a face, a posture, a wardrobe ("What country are you from?" Oh no. Take me home.), but it can get overwhelming to be alone among them.

I go into a Mister Donut and order a cup of coffee and a honey glaze at the counter. This is as American as it gets. Alone at a lunch counter in a strange city and on it one of those perfect tub-thick white cup and saucers with the two little delicate green stripes at the rim, and a doughnut on a paper napkin, wired out of your mind. It all looks so bright. "Wired!" She's wired me! I laugh out loud. I can't believe it'd never occurred to me before. Of course, she has to have known it all along. How funny. Amazing how the most obvious things escape your notice. Maybe the truth is exactly those things you don't notice. Maybe the aim to see and tell the truth is inherently futile, a contradiction in terms, and it's exactly those things about oneself and the world that are invisible because they are woven into one's fabric that are the truth. Just like a person can't see his own eyes. You search and search and search, and the truth, by definition, is exactly that which you don't find. You don't see the truth, you *are* the truth. "Habits of attention are reflexes of the complete character of an individual." And how could you notice your own habits of attention? By writing. Well, at their most profound level? It doesn't make any difference. That is the point. It's like Zen. The truth is in not straining for the truth, the truth is in effortlessness. The truth is in being, not trying. Aw hell, that doesn't leave me much to chew on.

This wing of fear brushes by again, that I've removed myself from the real arena. That I'm out here all caught up in doing unfunny routines featuring tricks with imaginary cards while over there, inside, where the real people are, there are things going on that matter because they're being performed from motives with a purity—with a purity from motives . . . with motives from a purity . . . from a purity with motives—that I've dissembled into rubble.

Never mind: Here I am with a coffee cup and together we are strong.

I go to a pay phone and call a cab to take me back to the motel.

15

When I come in, Chrissa is sitting on her bed writing postcards. The TV is on with the sound way down. I'm on too. It's all on. The room is dim and monochrome but for the lamp at her side and her in the warm light in her colorful clothes. All of it is buzzing and humming and crackling in my brain. She looks like an oil painting. She'd be entitled *Love Maker*. I remember her in her men's white shirt again, the first night we spent together. I yaw from the maw to take her in.

"Chrissa, it's so beautiful outside."

"This is a nice town."

"I've got a surprise." I reach into my pocket, separate the big speed packet from the dope, and pull it out.

"What's that?"

"It's speed—methadrine. Crystal meth."

"Where did you get that?"

"I went and saw somebody I know here. Have you ever done any of this stuff?"

"No, I don't think so."

"You ought to try it. You'll be glad you did. It's a stimulant. A—"

"I know what it is."

"You want to do a little?"

"Maybe."

"You'll like it, since you like coke. It's like coke but a little harder edged, and it lasts a long time. It just makes you feel incredibly good and makes your mind move fast. It's cool."

I'm sitting on the edge of my bed facing her, and I pull the drawer of the night table open and find a card with an S.F. map on it and take it out. I scrape some of the speed onto the card with a matchbook cover and make a line.

It looks as if she's going to use it. That makes me happy.

As I watch her I am suffused with this sudden sense of all the drug users in America at this moment. Our shadowy silent motel room becomes linked, like one among layers of transparent realities through which the drug light wends, to other rooms like it, icy little glowing shelters, comprising Grandma's house in the woods, deep in the sleeping dark and emptiness of the continent. Yes. Embarcation points. OUT: this way. They are my good and scary family, my kin and my constituency.

I let myself get sentimental watching her, as if she were asleep, as if I were God the parent. She sucks the drug up into one nostril, then the other. I seem to feel the compassionate sadness, the exhausted love, of a Buddha, for myself as well as for her, and everyone.

I don't want to go hide in the bathroom to get myself off, so I don't. I get out the new works, set myself up, and inject myself sitting at the little desk beside the TV. She's seen me do this many times in years past. It seems routine but sexy, like a small flirtation accepted, though I don't really know what she's thinking. I come back and sit on my bed.

"Chrissa, I've got to turn up the TV for a minute." It's caught my eye.

"OK."

There's a talk show on hosted by one of the least appealing men on television, talking to a sitcom star who's a rival for the title. I have to hear what they're saying. The host is a former third-tier crooner named Mel Farnum whose primary audience is aged women with flabby arms and too much leisure time. The guest is named Pete Vinton and he's a balding, chubby, and jovial little slickster who plays the household head of a twelve-child family on his popular weekly TV show. Pete's telling an anecdote from his youth.

"I was only thirteen, Mel, but the poster said it was educational. This was the forties. We were a lot younger when we were young then, weren't we? I know you were a lot younger, you hadn't even made your first nine-hundred trillion. Anyway, the poster said 'Half-man/Half-woman—Chris and Christine' in giant red letters. I was curious . . . but I was yellow. I worked up my courage. They let me in. It was a movie theater, but in those days they still had other attractions too—in fact, Mel, I think you were booked in with Jojo the Two-headed Dog for the following week. . . . There must have been about thirty of us in the audience. A man in a stained laboratory coat comes out on stage and gives us a somber lecture about human mutations and hermaphrodites in history. That's when they announced you were appearing soon. It's a joke, Mel. He's holding up a pamphlet describing this medical history, which they're selling in the lobby . . . Then a buxom but stern-looking lady in a nurse's uniform comes out down front and grabs a blanket that's bunched up on a wire in front of the stage. The wire runs above the middle aisle, and she starts pulling the blanket open along the thing, dividing the theater in half. The professor explains that this is to separate the gentlemen in the audience from the ladies, for the sake of propriety. Of course, there aren't actually any women there but this is getting more and more exciting and the suspense is building."

I'm fascinated. I can't believe how articulate the guy is and what a kinky story he's telling on prime-time national TV.

"Finally Dr. What's-his-name introduces Chris and Christine. This human person walks from the wings to the center of the stage and in profile it looks like an ordinary man with a beard. But when he turns to face the audience you see that he's divided down the middle. The beard ended under his nose and halfway across his chin, and even his clothes were simple and masculine on one side and more soft and flowery and feminine on the other. She pulls out her hair on the beardless side and it was long and shiny. I was amazed. And sure enough one side of her chest was large and the other flat . . ."

"You were thirteen?"

"Uh huh."

"What in heck were you thinking?"

"Well, I was in awe at the range and variety of God's creation. I was astonished. But that isn't the end of it . . . A few days later I was back at that theater to see a movie. Now, my dad had told me more than once that strange things can happen in dark movie houses. That it was possible that a man would sit by you and put his hand on your leg. And Dad told me that if that were ever to happen, I should just enunciate in a firm clear voice, 'Please take your hand off my knee.' I should be polite but emphatic, and speak loudly enough for the people around us to hear. Well, on that day it finally happened. I felt the hand of the man to my right come to rest on my knee. I was nervous, but I was prepared and I knew what to do. I turned toward him, the exact wording going through my mind. But, sure enough, who did I see beside me but Chris and Christine! I turned away. My mind was reeling. I was stumped. What could I do? I couldn't speak that way to a *star.*"

The studio audience roars with laughter. Mel asks, "Well, what did you do?"

"I sat there confused for a moment and then I got up and left the theater. . . . Later it occured to me and I couldn't help wondering: What would have happened if I'd been sitting on the other side of him?"

The audience laughs and laughs and starts clapping. I'm stunned.

"Were you listening to that?" I ask Chrissa.

She looks up. "Not really. A little." She's been writing postcards again, with a new intensity of concentration.

"This sitcom clown just gave a sympathetic description of a hermaphrodite on The Mel Farnum Show. Then he casually considered the possibility of having sex with him/her. It was far out. And nobody blinked. They were clapping for him on national TV. How strange. I think it means something."

Just then the phone rings. It's Steve from the bar. I have him hold on while I talk to Chrissa. I don't really feel like going out now. I get back on the phone and tell him we've had a long day and are kind of working now and I thank him and say maybe we could do it tomorrow if he has time. He's fine with that. I hang up.

Jesus, everywhere you turn there's sex. That's the cool thing about these stimulants: they tune you in to it. No matter where your mind takes you there's that underlying libidinal hum continuously stimulating your genitals until they poke through the noise and regain your attention. The methadrine undresses everything; it undresses words. Words are stripped to their naked purpose as plumage: more and more gorgeous but clearly intended to seduce. The intellect reaches in budding tendrils of words that push further and further into the light until they crack and bloom in fantastic sequences of lushest color but the single aim of it is to search out another orgasm and reproduce.

I talk to Chrissa. I riff on Pete Vinton and Chris and Christine. They've inspired me—Chrissa and I are the half-man/half-woman wrapped in our sideshow DeSoto pulling into towns across America, exhibiting ourselves and titillating the locals while secretly hoping to know them most immodestly. Maybe America is larger-minded than I've figured—not ignorant so much as awestruck and naïve, openminded. Pete's story restores vistas. I love the flavor of it—shady sweet and compassionate, not mean and bitter and cramped the way it could have been. It makes me think of Mark Twain, of Huck Finn. We discuss it.

I get frank. I tell Chrissa that I think she's boyish and I'm girlish. She's boyish in her narrow hips and androgynous wild-animal face and tangled hair and the pants she usually wears. And in her self-reliance and independence and the way she seems to target her sex partners rather than choose from among those that approach her. And I'm girlish in my softness and my emotional need, in my hairless chest and vanity, my weak chin and big lips, my longing, my love of beauty.

I know she's had sex with women. I haven't with men except for the usual teenage stuff—glamorous older juvenile delinqents from up the block who we're happy to let fuck us between the thighs. She asks me why not more, would I like to go with Steve to the gay bars? Why did I turn him down? Because it's too complicated, I say, and too predictable at the same time. It's like the Symbolist poets whose ennui kept ruling out all sorts of vaguely tempting experiences for themselves because they could just as easily imagine their outcome, so why bother. The actual experience would be too mundane and uncomfortable. I'm too old for it. Theoretically it holds some interest, but I can imagine too

bread houses lining the rising and dipping streets, an agreement that seems to hold among the inhabitants that they'll treat one another with tolerance and cheer, the cozy drama of the vista across rooftops in the undulating landscape that slopes down to the sea, the little shops full of new and old books and handmade decorations and pastries and sugary milk-whipped coffee, Gay-town and China bars.

We are greasy though, and as the day winds on and we wander the city, our patience wears thin. Bodily aches that follow from the exertion the speed induces start pushing through. I measure us out some more junk for the discomfort, but Chrissa's tolerance is so low it's too much for her and she gets sick. She looks awful: her face is drawn, her eyelids droop, and she has to stop and vomit in the gutter. The clarity dissolves. A weird thing has been happening with my mind all day too that can't be blamed on the drug, and it scares and preoccupies me. Every time I'm left alone and quiet for a minute I receive this charged image of a red-headed girl. I think I must have seen her in a dream this morning. She is as pale as milk with long curly red hair and I'm looking down at her where she is lying on her back. Her face is serene and intelligent and exquisitely beautiful, like some Pre-Raphaelite shepherdess, and she's very young. She looks like Mary Pickford. She's looking in my eyes and her naked upper body fills my field of vision but below her neck it's blurred because I'm looking in her face. Even so, the picture is overlain with the presence of her vagina from below—I know her naked legs are open—and it is shiny wet and even redder than her hair. It is offered to me in her eyes and it hovers there in my mind in a way that somehow feels heartbreaking but profoundly sexy, as sexually arousing as anything could possibly be. I keep seeing this. I can't keep my mind away from it. I want to have the sex with her that she is offering, and it's so overpowering that at one point in the afternoon I go into a men's room stall and start playing with myself in hopes of getting past it but the drugs make it impossible and I have to give up. It has me confused and disturbed and helpless. It's depressing that on the day when I'm finally wed to Chrissa I'm obsessed with someone else, even if she's imaginary. It makes me feel like I'm cheating. I thought that we'd come to the place where there would be no secrets between us but I'm not going to talk to her about this. It comes between us and makes me grouchy. It's like the snake in the garden.

But then, there is something delicious even about that. It makes me feel very old, but it doesn't reduce my love for Chrissa. In a way it makes me love us both even more deeply; the world is fabulously complex and our minds reflect it, continuously shifting and offering up new possibilities, and we wander through it hand in hand, trusting and surviving and doing our best. And then I think of her nipples and her eyelids and my heart pours open and I have to pull her to me and squeeze us into each other with all my power.

We live in timelessness this day and I talk to her about how it makes me despair for the book. Our experience makes writing and thought itself seem clumsy and irrelevant.

I think aloud and tell her how the interesting and worthy thing is to be shown that you know nothing, is to have the experience that suddenly makes everything you know fall away so that only awe remains. And what does language and thought do to that? Make it awful. No, but that's too easy to be true itself. Language is what you make of it. It is the car for our car, that I get to fully design and then drive where I choose. And if I want to get out and walk for a while I can do that, too. There aren't any limits to it.

As the day winds down and dusk falls, we work our way back to the motel. There in our room we are like damp baby birds with brittle bones drawn back to the nest of our bedclothes. I take another tiny line of dope and we smoke some grass. We are dead tired but still exalted, holding each other in the warm and cool folds of covers, eyes closed and open, imagery flowing across and through us as we drift in safety and danger. Every motion seem fated. I say that aloud, "Every motion seem fated." I let myself not question the love, and she does the same. Slowly, slowly, and in lubricated fits and starts, we fall asleep.

17

I wake up first in the morning and I feel as if I've been beaten up, so I immediately do another small line of dope. It is weird and kind of scary to wake up in Chrissa's bed. Without the speed I don't know how we'll maintain this new level we've reached. I have some left but I know better than to get us started on it again. It would weaken us, it would be too squalid, Chrissa would not go for it. Anyway, the dope helps. It's calming and takes away the worst of my aches.

I get in the other bed with my notebook and look over the books I found in the used bookstore. There are three of them, a cool old Modern Library edition of Baudelaire, Ted Berrigan's beautiful little Corinth paperback collection of poems *Many Happy Returns,* and the first edition of Philip Caputo's *A Rumor of War,* a great fearsome memoir of Vietnam which I've been looking for for a while. I examine my finds; they give me such pleasure. Their power is mysterious. The Baudelaire is old. The pages are yellowing at the edges—they look like mushroom meat—and the cover, the color of thin blood, is chipping off at the binding. The page leaves are heavy though, and the Times Roman print a distinguished letterpress. It has copyright dates of 1919 and 1925 and includes three separate effusions of intro: an ode by Swinburne, a long biographical essay, and an editor's note ("Mr. Arthur Symon's translation of some of the prose poems is a most beautiful adventure in psychological sensations . . ."). The prefaces and introductions and epigraphs are quaint in their self-important formality and their dated phraseology, but they are moving in their innocence and sincerity and in the very way they are helplessly pinned to their era by their styles and attitudes while they confidently rattle on as if they're going to live forever.

Meanwhile, the translations themselves are wonderful: the prose, which comprises over half the book, is perfect, and while the poems are more problematic, with lots of extravagant language and compromises in meaning forced by the straining for rhymes and other difficulties in transferring from one language to another, the results are not all that far from giving the effect the writer must have had on his original readers, which is thrilling to sense. After all, Baudelaire is voluptuous and extravagant and inclined to sacrifice a lot for "aesthetic" effect. And though he cultivated his antibourgeois ennui and pessimism, he was starved for appreciation. I identify with him a lot and I think he would have been pleased with the respect he's given in this book, a mass-market volume, precursor of pocket paperbacks. I identify with him so much that I think the book is funny—to me he is half a fraud, and he's clearly managed to put something over on these guys as he desperately needed to and I'm happy for him. The volume represents him perfectly. All he really had was his taste and his longing, his longing for the infinite. He refused to be intimidated by conventions—he made the case for the way he actually felt and saw things, as ugly—perverse—and hopeless as it was. He had no vitality, he was beaten, and all he produced were fragments and misshapen imitations of his idols such as Poe, but he took himself seriously and was smart enough and determined enough to be acknowledged that he managed to make a virtue of his pathetic weaknesses; he made them his purpose and his identity and it worked. He was brave. I'm glad for him and his success encourages me. As I page carefully through the fragile book, I can feel him and he is noble and the book itself is subversive and fascinating. His example gives me hope.

And then there is the Berrigan and the Vietnam, so different from the Baudelaire, but so good themselves. They are three magical treasures. I look at them in a little heap on the bed and they are my wealth, my security. I feel like a miser for a moment and that is a little creepy but I know I'm not really infected with the mania that way—it's just that I love and cherish my favorite books. They are the most generous friends.

I start writing about them in my notebook and it feels like I could go on forever. Love is stimulating. But I'm too wasted. I try to get down the strongest ideas, from which the others spring, but it all swirls off into the mists where I'm not inclined to go tracking, and I put down my pencil and curl up comfortably and doze off.

When I wake up again, Chrissa is still sleeping. I want to do some more speed, but I think I should at least hold off until I've eaten something. My stomach feels like a grinding crevasse somewhere on the edge of the earth. Even though the speed has suppressed our appetites so that we've hardly eaten anything for 36 hours, I'm still not really hungry. I just feel this sensation which I intellectually recognize as a sign that food could be of use. So I go into the bathroom and clean up a little and then go out to get some eggs.

Thank God for drugs, I say to myself walking through the motel parking lot. What would I do without them? There's something for everything. They keep things new and they give me my adventures. I feel like a winning athlete. I'm sore but tall on the way to my San Francisco breakfast.

I end up doing the rest of the speed after I eat and it puts me on my own. Chrissa doesn't have much patience for me. I hunch over the maps, turn the TV up and down, scratch in my notebook, zigzagging from task to task, aware of Chrissa's disillusionment and disapproval but helpless and defiant in the grip of the drug and my compulsions. She gets testy with me, she gets sarcastic, and I swipe back instantly and meanly, my allegiance to drugs stronger than any other loyalty. Every once in a while I'll be able to make her laugh and these are the high points of the afternoon. We've gone from newlyweds to trapped old married couple in one day.

She goes out by herself for a long time. She wants to get away from me and anyway I'm too paranoid to face the light. I keep the curtains closed. My face feels scratchy and I can smell my armpits but every time I consider the shower something distracts me. Anyway, it would be too scary in there alone. I'm seeing things out of the corners of my eyes and talking to myself. The phone rings once and startles me so badly I think my heart has split, and waiting for the ringing to stop is like waiting for my execution. I write and write in my notebook but I can't keep up with my thoughts. One sentence will unfurl and scroll out until not only have I lost any sense of where it's going but I've forgotten where it started, and I'm pressing so hard with the pencil and making so many erasures that the page is like a battleground. I scratch my itchy head and look around to see what to do next.

I want to go fuck Kathy but I can't bring myself to leave. I can't have her come over of course because Chrissa might walk in. I call her and draw her into phone sex but, unable to come, I jerk the skin back and forth over the head of my dick until it bleeds and then in the middle of this Chrissa starts to unlock the door. Fortunately I have the chain on, but opening the door I'm some awful Igor, completely witless and inappropriate for any purpose but horror.

It is another short long day, endless every moment but over in the blink of an eye, and the other way around. I am very glad to be sleepy by midnight but it takes a thick line that nearly finishes the dope and three more hours before I'm just starting to doze. We've agreed we'll leave San Francisco in the morning.

18

The next day is awful. I'm short tempered in my misery and Chrissa resents it. I use the last little bit of dope in the morning and then can't reach Kathy all day as I mope and curse around the motel. Beneath the dreadful discomfort and exhaustion is a fluttering panic at the prospect of leaving town without junk that is really a weak defense against recognizing the more profound panic at my dependency itself. I'm pretending to have a broken wing to save my offspring.

We are paying heavily for our one day of bliss.

I want to drive to Las Vegas from here, but the little leverage I still have with Chrissa dwindles as it gets later in the day. Vegas is way south, east of Los Angeles, and by the afternoon I have to agree that Reno, which is much closer to San Francisco, is the only choice. I finally reach Kathy but she hardly has anything left until tomorrow. I buy the one bag she has and finally Chrissa and I leave town.

It's good to be back in the car. Chrissa drives.

We drive out of San Francisco toward Stockton with the idea of taking a slightly roundabout route to avoid the boring super-highways. I rest my head against the cool window of the DeSoto and let my mind be as quiet as I can against the streaming western view of California hills.

Chrissa and I are each alone in adjoining psychological cubicles in the front seat and I don't mind. I am peaceful and content. Her anger is a wall between us but since I want to be alone anyway it's all right with me. It's only when the wall crumbles around some pointed remark of hers that the peace is disturbed. We cross the farm-plush Sacramento Valley driving toward the Sierra Nevadas. I doze and sleep and don't thoroughly wake up until we're coming down out of the mountains into Nevada just fifty or sixty miles south of Reno. Soon we're winding and speeding through the desert: brown hills, sand, and emptiness. It isn't really empty though. The time of day keeps changing and the sky is huge and the clouds keep changing, too. Furthermore, we're here.

Chrissa is driving very fast which is not a good idea in a car this old, but she isn't going to attend my wisdom. Speed does feel correct: Everything in view is so large and long stretches of road are perfectly straight. You can't get away from it; no matter how fast you go it remains the same and there to consider, so why not?

As usual when faced with a landscape the major features of which aren't manmade, I reflexively wonder what it would have been like to be here before anyone else. Big mongrel America. No poetry in our name, except, yes, that mongrel start. The United States of some Italian vagrant. I think of the Indians whom we'd misnamed as well. How embarrassing. Yes, we are vulgur brutes. But poetry is the real world and we just its dumb misunderstanders. Death is just a dumb human idea. Every drama, every conflict, is continuously played out everywhere and in all time one way or another. It's snobbery, which itself is a kind of ignorance, a kind of xenophobia, to imagine a culture as brutish. We're just another one of poetry's ideas. The mind a kind of toy. A malleable thing that local poetry shapes and then it is given to one to try and keep it corresponding to all it encounters. That is the game. We mistake ourselves as discrete in time.

The car speeds through the desert scrub and I try to apologize to Chrissa for my reckless selfishness. "It's my nature, Chrissa, and I suffer from it as much as anyone . . . I want to change."

"That's boring."

"Why?"

"Because it's perfectly predictable. It never changes. You've been saying that your complete life. I'm not your school prefect or your counselor or your mother. You think you can put yourself in the position to your friends of a little boy who will be forgiven everything. All you think of is yourself. The truth is every relationship is a trade, a bargain, even the most loyal ones, but you are completely selfish. And you can't get away with it forever.

You are a thief of emotions. And eventually anyone but the most abject will see what you're giving them is much smaller than what they're getting."

She must have been thinking pretty hard while I slept. "You're right. I can't defend myself," I tell her.

I'm hurt but even then I still take a shred of pleasure in being the center of attention and that makes me feel crazy. I watch the desert go by, feeling my swirling brain click in habitual patterns that aren't useful in the circumstances. It resembles sulking, but it's really just that I am at a loss. I don't know an honest place to go from here. I feel awful but I also feel that familiar defiance and mildly self-pitying sense of release from some troublesome human contact. The silence in the car resumes.

The silence in the car resumes.

The silence in the car resumes. "The silence in the car resumes," I mutter.

Chrissa laughs. "What are you doing, writing the book?"

I hadn't really quite realized I was saying it aloud, but, "Yeah," I say, "Not exactly . . . That was weird." I laugh too. "Chrissa laughs," I say, and we're both laughing. We giggle in the speeding car.

After a while I start talking. "God, I love those two words *Chrissa laughs*. That sentence. Maybe I'll call the book *Chrissa Laughs*. It'll be a twentieth-century Mona Lisa. But of course she wasn't laughing. Are there any great portraits laughing, showing teeth? I don't think so. Why is that, do you think? Even if you try to imagine a painting of a person laughing it's a little grotesque. It must be because the teeth and open mouth become the center of attention. Laughs—isolated laughs—have more in common with each other than anything they say about the person laughing. A laughing portrait is a portrait of a laugh, not the laugher. Like that Frans Hals. In paintings anyway—there's 'Garbo laughs'. It's because paintings have no time, or they're frozen. You can do it in movies or books, because you can see what produced the laugh and why it matters and the consequences . . . Well, scratch that. But still, *Chrissa Laughs*, I like that. I could live with that.

" 'The silence in the car resumes.' I just heard the sentence in my head. And then I was wondering about it. I was wondering how long it would be any good. Just a simple sentence like that. It's the 'car' that will probably get obsolete, and then the spellings. And then somebody else will have to write this book. Everything has to continually get done all over again. Artists imagine they're doing something definitive, or for all time, and of course it's not true, and then there are those who think everything's already been said and find that discouraging which is just as ridiculous. Just the way a child has to completely learn about life for itself all over again, without the benefit of its parents' experience, every generation does too. You know what I mean? The same insights have to be had, the same various strains—flavors—of types of beauty and knowledge and wisdom must be discerned and concocted all over again in the mixture that suits the given time and place. That's not discouraging, it's interesting. Unless you don't think it's interesting to be human, which I must admit is an idea that's crossed my mind. But that idea itself is about as human as you can get and should be rejected at once."

Chrissa laughs again, for which I am grateful.

I'm going over the edge. "Chrissa, maybe you're not Christine, maybe you're Christ. And you're forgiving me. Did Christ ever laugh? I'll have to look it up in the Bible. Or we can ask people on the trip. Yeah, I was just thinking about how names are their own . . . inarguable . . . ultimate poetry, beautiful and perfect like cave paintings—that aren't the work of anyone but of generations . . . Maybe you're Christ and I'm Christ's goofy errant sidekick—scum but with a berning hardt. And I'm going to save your life or sacrifice myself for you or something . . ."

"Slow down, Billy. You took a wrong turn there."

"You don't wanna be Christ?"

"No."

"Neither did he."

"Stop it. Cool off."

"OK." She doesn't want to talk anymore. My mind is still going, thinking what I really am is Mlle. Christ's performing dog. "He cured a woman vassal's slave but he could not cure the clown of the need to slap his dog. And when the messengers went back to the house, they found the slave well but the dog dead." I don't want to resent her though. I know that most of all she can't stand me imagining her into all these roles my condition needs. Fuck, I am fucked up. The sunset sure looks great though.

"Look at that," she says. "Is it ours?"

I feel like she's stabbed me in the heart. Does she mean our time is ending?

"What do you mean?"

"I mean we've got to stop thinking about ourselves and look around us. We're supposed to be working."

"I know. I'm working."

The sunset *is* amazing over the hills beside us, reaching all the way around the sides of the car. She is calling attention to the Father. Purple climbing on pink and green with little mosaic checkerboards of mown and puzzled diamond inset, and faded tapestries interwoven along, in grainy streams upon which one could just discern the motif of crimson-mouthed and grinning long-nosed golden hounds wildly pursuing a rabbit with blazing cigars of dynamite amouth. The hounds have legends shaven in their flaring hides. I can just make out a motto and it reads, "Donut take and not the tear conceal." Was it tare or teer? Donut or do not? Fringes of plaid that stretch from pole to pole are fraying and all the chilly world is blurred occluded in, as ruffled wind makes giant shields of snowy chips that mount like seashells of iridescent mail upon the desk of shoulders. They climb like masses of beetles become spirit in the effort, beautiful enough to let you sleep. And all rejoice in silence, quoth the missing fowl. In silence . . . Heretofore unheard of . . .

19

We pull into Reno early that night. I am surprised at how little it costs to stay at a casino in the middle of town. Soon it's apparent that in Reno all the essentials are cheap. They are bait to flatter and keep you and make money seem trivial so you'll spend it gambling. They even hide the clocks.

Though our cheap room is tiny it has all the trimmings—thick shag carpet, obnoxious little Western painting, and five kinds of soap—and it feels like a stall in a slaughterhouse. The whole town is an insinuated insult. Everywhere, inescapably, you are being treated as dumb livestock.

I had a small idea of Nevada as an interesting place where victimless vice is freely indulged. An old-fashioned cowboy saloon to the nation where the poker tables are always open, the girls all want to take you upstairs, the booze flows freely, and no one will arrest you for any of it. Almost enlightened. It'd be all open fun.

In fact, the place is utterly ugly and banal-sinister. The apotheosis of the crooked whore, the most cynical of con games. The neon slapping you on the back with its big grins, little promises shouted and whispered at you from everywhere, while in the back room, behind the false walls, the musclebound hunchbacks with their brains wired to ancient death-circuits of mindless dominance wait with knives in hand, slavering and chill. Everyone here is either dead meat or a vulture.

Stuck in it, one helplessly wonders whether this might really be the underlying reality of human existence. Looking around, I say to Chrissa, "I'm glad I'm not tripping." Everyone's reflexive dream of something for nothing, everyone's self-centered universe, susceptibility to transparent flattery, all our pathetic weaknesses are being addressed here, stroked and caressed in the most vulgar style, encouraged and then exploited for cash. It's offensive to be taken for such a fool, but it's so basic, so pathetically typical of us to fall for it. I'll give you all my money if you'll tell me I'm important.

I am tired and grouchy. I'm tense and worried because my drug supply is almost gone. I know what I'll be facing tomorrow, out on the streets searching for a supply from the locals, but that doesn't stop me from doing the last but one, tiny morning-line of it.

The line I do in the bathroom takes away my sniffles and muscle-poison but doesn't improve my frame of mind. I am pissed and disgusted. I turn on the TV. Some moronic sitcom is on. A bunch of self-satisfied teenagers wallowing in canned and unearned laughter, enough to make you puke. I'd like to take that fat one and swing her from her hair at the cute one so they both split like the overripe vegetables they are and let the bugs eat em. Then a break for advertising, which of course is equally repulsive. An ominous sentimental "public service" picture of some lost and murderous waif. "Get her off the streets . . ." American streets, the horrible fate . . .

All of this is pushing me far away but I don't have anywhere to go, so I am squeezed. Chrissa won't take me in. What the fuck am I doing here, I wonder. I wish I was back in New York. The money and the car and the credit card and air-conditioning and Chrissa and all of this is less than shit if I don't have the drugs to keep me straight. Can't you understand this? Why are you in my way!?

Fuck shit piss. Another night ahead. The traffic outside, the noise, those liquid, impossible colored lights, this room, this insensible room in Reno, Nevada, none of them, none of it but greasy crusts of encroaching death, time, huge gritty flakes, strata of awful time-pastry blinding and enwrapping me until it tastes and stinks of sweat, of rank and wasted waiting-time, just stink and shit and vomit. And no one anywhere but *agh*. I've known this situation so many times before, though, I know it so well, I know there is nothing to do but endure it. Complaints or violence will get me nowhere, and anyway I am too weak to bother.

Chrissa doesn't know what I'm going through. I just tell her the city puts me in a bad mood and that I'm sorry. I fear the night ahead but it's with the kind of unbearable but borne resignation that a soldier feels at the front. I do the last pathetic thread-thin seam of junk that I'd intended to save and call room service while I can still eat. There is plenty of booze in the minirefrigerator and a little bit of grass left.

Chrissa still thinks I've beaten my habit. I half thought so myself. It might even be true and what I am experiencing is no worse than a mild case of the flu mixed with insomnia, and the real problem is my fear of unfamiliar direct reality, but that doesn't matter—I can't continue in this condition. The mission that precedes all others and makes them possible is the quest for dope.

For tonight I just withdraw to the bed and drink and smoke and wait, watching TV. I tell Chrissa I think I'm getting a cold. My nose is running and I have little fits of sneezing. When she falls asleep I leave the TV on low and switch back and forth between it and my books, but of course none of it speaks to me. I think I can sleep before too long, but I'm not looking forward to waking up. Once I turn the lights out I lie twisting in the bed, finally dozing toward dawn for a few deadly thin hours. The bed gets wet with sweat.

Around eight-thirty in the morning, I take a shower and go out because I don't know what else to do. There aren't many people on the street but an outrageously high proportion of them are drunk. It's obvious as soon as I've walked a few blocks that I'm going to get nowhere. It is too early and it isn't New York. I have no idea how dope is distributed here. I am more and more demoralized but I just armor myself in a junkie's hopeless resignation and keep walking in circles. The blaring sunlight is painful and offensive again.

I keep coming across drive-through wedding chapels. Pawnshops and casinos. Pornography galore. Who is here? Who the fuck would be here? I don't want to know. It would be cruel and discourteous to know, like staring at a burn victim. What is there to know about them but deformity and pain? They have their dignity, but it isn't my metaphor. It just makes me sad and crazy and scared, scared to see myself in them. The people here make me itch like bugs, they bug me, I just want to scratch them away and get some dope and get fucking high.

I don't want to impose on Chrissa, revealing myself in this condition, so I keep killing time outside. I buy a newspaper and sit on a bench in the intensifying sunlight for an hour or two, smoking cigarettes and reading. I'm feeling worse and worse: My nose keeps leaking, I'm sweating that familiar unhealthy cheese-sweat that isn't like real sweat but some awful smelly inner ugliness leaching up and seeping out through the skin, my bowels twist, and my muscles are pinched from within.

As the morning wears on, I finally spot some of the types on the street who might be able to help me. The street kids and runaways and petty hoods. Skinny boy-men with down mustaches, and stray girls in makeup and cutoffs; pimples, scowls, tattoos, and second-hand clothes.

Finally I get up and get started with the idea of finding one of these guys I can approach. I walk around, surreptitiously eyeing the occasional street corner scattering of my targets, feeling more and more like a highschool geek, like the guy who is going to be included last. I pull my plates of shell tightly across myself but it makes walking problematic. I feel like I'm having motor difficulties—I can't find a way of holding myself that isn't stiff and awkward. I want to have a demeanor, an attitude, that will inspire confidence in this juvenile trailer-camp trash, my brothers, but I feel like a mark, I feel like a sucker and I know it shows.

I am too old and green and dumb and needy. I know the money in my pocket is theirs, it isn't mine. This attitude is fatal, self-fulfilling, but like a grunt who is sure he's gonna be offed on patrol, I can't shake the feeling. Worse, it suddenly hits me, they probably think I'm a gay guy trying to build up steam to talk to them. Shit. I want to swagger, I want to be bored and curse and street-knowing, I want to speak their language, but I don't have the resources. I'm only beat and desperate and spastic.

I stand across the street from a little gang who are gathered in front of a tacky clothing store. I'm hoping one of them will approach me the way he would in New York. They ignore me. I can see that I'm making them a little nervous as I stand there minute after minute after minute with no purpose. Finally one of them breaks off from the group and starts away down the street. I follow him on the other side and then cross as soon as I can. I walk up alongside of him.

"Yo," I say.

He just looks at me.

"Hey, man," I say, "I'm from out of town and I'm fucked up. I'm gettin junk sick and I gotta cop. I'm trying to figure out how to do that here. It's worth some cash if you'd help me out."

He keeps walking and I keep up.

"See," I ask. I flash him my track marks.

"Where're you from?" he asks.

"New York."

"I was there once. So many chicks. You ever go to George's?"

"George's?"

"Yeah, it's a bar in the Village."

"Never heard of it."

"You oughtta go there some time. Rockin place."

"I'll remember that." Fuck shit piss. "What's the scene around here for dope?"

"It's not New York. I could probably get you some mushrooms."

"I noticed it's not New York. I need junk, man."

"I could look into it."

"I'll make it worth your while."

"I'd have to get back to you later."

"OK."

"I'll need some car fare . . ."

I reach into my pocket and squeeze a twenty off the thin fold, crease it twice more in the palm of my hand, and slide it into his. He looks down at it.

"Where you stayin?"

"At a hotel, but you can't call me there. Can I find you someplace?"

"Yeah, I hang out at the Hardee's on Fourth Street. It's right around the corner. How much you want?"

"What—dimes? Grams? At least a hundred dollars worth, maybe more, depending on how good it is."

"All right. I'll look into it. Come by Hardee's around three o'clock and I'll try to help you out."

"Great, man." I say, "And listen—percodans, morphine, codeine, dilaudid, any kinda narcotic'll do if there ain't no real dope around."

"I'll see what's out."

We part ways and I start the trudge back to the hotel.

20

It's demoralizing to realize that everything about yourself is an act. The pretense that anything matters but dope is clearly a luxury for me.

I decide to go into an anonymous little bar I spot on the street. It's cool and dark inside and smells of disinfectant and cigarette smoke like half the bars in America. Reno does have natives. The only thing that locates the room is the slot machines along the walls. I sit on a stool and order a scotch and beer.

I feel dizzy for a second. My heart expands and I'm trying to yawn, my eyes watering. I stretch, like I'm waking up, and I see stars for a second. The top of my inner skull empties out and my head floats up to the ceiling, and then it all sifts and collapses and I'm sitting on the stool again, my muscles tingling as if they are thawing. I don't feel terribly bad. In fact I have an idea that I might really be able to tough through the withdrawal and beat my habit. The barroom looks very clear and sharp-edged and real. My pupils are open. I can see myself in the mirror behind the bar. I look furtive and minor among the bleary crosshatch and bottles and doubled space. I take a drink of whiskey.

Suddenly I remember poetry. I've been reading the Berrigan. I feel sorry for my poor self. I remember poetry and I understand it. It is something I have left. Did I leave it or do I have it left? Oops, I'm fucking up again. Return to track, you idiot. Poetry is the only, the only connective tissue. I want to make it so bad, because I love it so much. Something in me could do it. That thing can't be ruined, it can only be misplaced or hidden. The poetry's in the pity. Who said that? Wilfred Owen? Christmas on earth. Mercy. Well it is, but the pity has a castle the size of the whole universe with rooms of gaping terror, clear buckets to place your face in, and doo wop, etc., etc. Maybe I can't live in it but I can visit and my grungy half-blindness can still press to convey its clear correlation, its incarnation, in words and I'm bound to make it now and then if I insist and persist, if I'm humble. I want to cry. Why all these costumes? Is it possible to be otherwise? Maybe not and I am just too soft now. But whatever it takes if your eye stays on the prize. It doesn't matter whose prize it is. That's what makes it poetry. That's why they came up with muses, the whole point is giving up yourself. Ogh ugh, set me free of this ego-flesh. I am such a scared person, so scared to be seen, set me free of this, please, let me forget me. I'll never, ever, ever be able to do it. Oh well, forget about it.

Devise. I have to laugh at myself. How long has it been since I had methadone? Three days? I should be feeling the worst of it now. Except for the last two days and a couple of lapses it'd been weeks since I did dope. If this is as bad as it gets, I might be able to pull through. My nose is running and I gag easily, I know I won't be sleeping very well, but maybe I can make it. God, what a great idea. Maybe I can come out the other side. But will I be able to do any work? This isn't a vacation.

It feels like ice is breaking up in my muscles. I stretch and stand back from the stool and see stars again. I sit back up and finish my drink and order another. The sharp fumes and flavor of the scotch are great.

An old guy with a pockmarked nose and clouded glasses has sat on a stool one away from me. When I get my second drink he catches my eye.

"How ya doin," he rasps.

"Oh, I'm improvin. How bout you?"

"Same as ever, which could be worse."

I wait for him to say something else but he doesn't. I ask him, "Ever know any junkies?"

"Junkies? Dope fiends? Some. I knew a couple. Knew one real good. Bill."

"What?"

"I said I knew this one junkie real good."

"Bill?"

"That was his name. He was a musician."

I shiver inside and my eyes start to water. "What happened to him?"

"He passed away."

"He was a good friend of yours?"

"He was a goddamned junkie and that says it. He messed with my old lady at the time. Took her away from me and made her into a whoor. He ud talk a dollar off a dime. But he was scum. We all was sorry he died cuz then we couldn't kill him."

I laugh one vertical ha but he doesn't say anything else. I look at him, root-dark old man akimbo, like a flung pile of chopped wood, with his rutted sinewy face like a place where the root is torn open to the wall, thick repaired cloudy grey-barred glasses balanced in the soft violence there like some kind of child's joke, streaky dirt-shiny sprout clod of hat atop, and I feel fear from the spine that knobs the back of my neck to my bowels. I stand from the stool and walk straight out the door and from there directly back to the hotel room. My eyes are watering and I am dazed.

"Chrissa, I'm scared."

"What do you mean?"

I sit on the edge of the bed. She's sitting on the edge of hers facing me. I can only get a shallow breath. Finally I hook a half-caught lungful and exhale.

"I've gotta tell you—I'm not really clean. I'm junk sick right now. I was just out on the street trying to find something here. It was horrible. I'm scared. I'm really scared. I thought I'd got myself clean. I meant to, I tried to, I thought I'd done it . . ."

She isn't saying anything. What are all these silences from people today? It's like I'm talking in a void or a mirror or to rubber and it bounces off them and sticks to me or to the straining-to-listen dead or to a judge, and the challenge of translating a thing that is whole and complete in the brain into strings of words is overwhelming and I keep stumbling and searching ineffectually.

I continue, "I guess I knew it might not be so simple, that it'd catch up with me, that there'd have to be some payment . . . But, fuck, what difference does it make? I'm sorry Chrissa. See how my nose is running? I feel so weak. And I won't be able to sleep or eat. Shit."

"Is there anything I can do for you?"

"If you would not be mad at me it would be a great thing."

"I'm not mad at you."

"I'm scared that I'm gonna cop and I'm scared that I'm not gonna cop."

"I know, I mean I see. I understand . . . I'll help you, Billy. You've got to try and not get anything."

"But how can I do any of this work if I'm sick? I'm not good for anything. I'm a total mess. I feel so weak right now that I could cry. I'd like to cry."

"Go ahead and cry. Come over here."

I step over and turn around and sit beside her and she pulls my head down to her shoulder. It kind of hurts my neck. She lets herself sink backward and we bounce slightly on the mattress once before she swings her legs up. I lift mine up, too, and we scrunch over more toward the center of the bed and I lie with my head on her chest. It feels strange, me being so much bigger than her. Everything feels strange and puppetlike for a moment and I want to vomit.

"Doesn't my breath smell bad?"

"It smells like whiskey."

"I'm gonna mess up your blouse." My nose is running and my eyes are watering.

"Forget about it. Just do what you need to."

I close my eyes. How can she be giving me this? She has her hand in my hair and at my temple and with my eyes closed I press my head into the firmness and softness where her ribs fuse just below her throat. In that position in the darkness behind my eyelids I feel so alone and exhausted but so comforted but so lost, and I don't care that I'm sorry for myself because I am so weak and so grateful to Chrissa I feel us blowing, tumbling like leaves in the giant cut and she is letting me cling to her and my heart clinches and clinches dry as a rock and then she says "I love you"—how can she do that?—and still I'm not crying. My mind says, What does she mean? What's her purpose in saying that? She's trying to help and it sounds wrong. But when I don't say anything back and her words become some awful empty childish mansion, finally the sadness precipitates and a tear drips out and then I cry and things get real again or we return to the script or whatever you'd call it and I sob and slobber and soak her shirt with snot and she is loving me like a beautiful mother who'd be willing and able to have exquisite sex with me, her child, if that's what it took though it's the last thing either of us are interested in but the sobs are great but it is so far too late that it's awful but it's so far too late that it gets even greater and more awful until I even cry myself to a kind of sleep for a minute before I wake up sicker than ever and at a total dead-tired loss and self-sufficient weariness that I share with her and that is tough and good. I want to tell her I am sorry again, but I am sick of being sorry. There is no percentage in it.

21

I decide to tell her what she can expect.

"Here's what's going to happen: I'm going to be in a bad mood. I'm going to be tense and impatient and irritable. That's the worst part where you're concerned. I'll try to keep it in check, I'll do my best, but you've got to not take it personally."

As I talk I feel stronger. Withdrawal becomes an ordeal that I know will come to an end, like a punishment, a specific sentence, rather than overall impending doom. When I can see it in that light I'm powerful and I have hope. But it's hard to maintain. Chrissa's presence helps and so does the simple physical difficulty of copping in this strange town.

I tell her about the guy I'm supposed to meet at three and right away, in the first hour, my resolve, our mission, loses its simplicity and purity. I won't unequivocally agree not to go meet the guy. Right away I'm removed from my voice. As I make my case to her I squirm inside, alone and despairing and defiant in my infantile righteousness as I hear the sound of fuzzy self-deceptive falsehoods. I am trying to be honest and logical, insisting that I might be able to get some valiums from the guy which would let me have a little sleep and make the days more bearable while this is going on, but something in me knows that if he has dope I'll buy it. Just the discomfort of arguing with her, of exposing my self-manipulation, makes me wish I were alone again, has me making the case for dope again in my head and not telling her. But this is all familiar and I stay there with her and, as three approaches, I tell her how I don't trust myself and explain the tricks my mind keeps playing on me to justify using. This is a relief and the first crisis passes.

I drink all day and watch TV, good for nothing. I sweat, I

yawn, I gag, I have diarrhea, my nose runs and my eyes water, my muscles pain as if they were mixed with strips of torn aluminum, and I find excuses to send Chrissa out three times so I can noisily spurt shit or jerk off in privacy, but the worst part is the exhaustion and anxiety. I cry, not from the discomfort, but sentimentally, vulnerable from weakness and exposure, self-pity, out of helpless empathy with the poor in all things, and amazement at every kindness: that kind of exhaustion. The anxiety level is outrageous. Every gauged moment I want out of my skin, and brain and being. Because something is trying to kill me. I want out of this deadly hyperconsciousness of physical sequence, of myself in space and time, this awareness of threat. And then, inexplicably, it ebbs for an instant. I am so tired and somehow my attention will find a fissure and leak into some other place relieving the pressure for a measureless moment before the spew can refill the cavities and I'm twitching again. And in that moment I realize how trivial it all is and I talk to Chrissa, encouraging her and myself. After all I'm not really dying. There are people in much worse pain. It's the low, black cloud of nameless evil, oblivious forces of mockery, and graceless, worse-than-death, crashing, turbulent, relentless anxiety that is the problem. The crying feels good, or it feels better than not crying. I remember this anxiety. Isn't it my character? I can't survive it. I rack my brain to remember if there is a me that can endure it, if I'd ever been otherwise before heroin. I fear not, but Chrissa knows differently, and I'm OK for a little while. I am really scared of when she'll have to go to sleep and I'll be alone again, nailed in a sickening spotlight . . .

The night comes and, you know, I don't want to write about it because I don't want to live it again. Basically, it goes on and on. It's like watching the paint dry only you're the wall and you're full of termites and as soon as you're almost dry they paint you again. And it'll never stop because nobody cares, nobody even notices: Painting a wall's no crime. All right, all right.

Sometimes I "laugh." Just as an experiment and for the sake of rebellion and exercise. There isn't any amusement to it. It is only a noise and a little facial muscular thing. It doesn't serve much purpose. It only returns a scary echo but it reminds me I am there underneath it all. Basically it's insane, but it's some kind of soothing.

I jerk off again a couple of times: It's the last instant gratification left. My dick is in an odd state. It's ultrasensitive and numb at the same time. It comes even before it gets fully hard, but it's perfunctory, strictly mechanical, like some safety device in a dam releasing overflow. All my fluids are overflowing. Sweat, snot, shit, and tears. They've been dry for so long.

I cry at every kindness on TV. In the middle of the night in Reno silently crying at the spontaneous family-feeling captured in a TV telephone commercial.

Finally, a couple of hours after the sun comes up, I doze a little. It's a surface sleep that comes in irregular little tiles but it's better than treasure. The final installment of it actually seems to refresh me a little, but hope and try as I might I can't regain it, and I sit up in bed and light a cigarette. I feel a crunching hunger that seems a good sign too. If I am going to be able to eat I can't be too bad off. I go and run a bath for myself.

The hot bath undoes my muscles, steaming their twitching lumps out for moments, but, like slime-mold slugs, the crowds of separated muscle cells seem to slink along the viscera and knot together again farther down the fibered night soil. I smoke and read a magazine, grateful for the arrival of day, with its veneer of activity against which I might blend in a little. My sleepless, endless night, in which the isolation seemed so conspicuous, is mercifully fading already, exactly like a nightmare. I feel like I can eat, and I feel human: not like a sickness itself but like one who has a sickness. I have a rush of hope.

Chrissa is stirring outside and I call out, "Good morning!" My words sound foreign after the long night, but the "Good morning" she calls back is like luck itself.

We go out for breakfast and even though the food has no taste it doesn't make me throw up. I tell her how the previous night has been, even including the masturbation. She tells me I can wake her up at any time and we laugh but it gives me a strange feeling. She seems really sincere in her willingness to completely subsume herself in my needs and I don't know exactly how to take it. I decide the trade must be that she really wants me clean and it's that simple. I try to tell her how glad I am for her kindness. I do want to be worthy of her. She says not to worry about that, to just think of her as being there for my purposes, like a slave or a pet or a robot. That that would be her happiness. I feel strange again, but she insists she really means it. I reach across the table and kiss her on the mouth and she responds to everything I do with my tongue like a schoolgirl hungry for it and when I stop she just accepts my lead. I think she must have made some kind of resolution to herself.

We decide to leave Reno that day.

The car's air-conditioning doesn't work, but the dry air streaming in through the windows feels good as I lie in the rhythmically coursing sofa of a backseat. I am some wounded bank robber being carried by my faithful partner across the desert.

I watch the little odd-shaped arcs of sky I can see from my angle and I squirm and twist in the dryness. The pulsing buzzing vibratility of the seat is greatly calming to the muscles, though, and I doze in that familiar feverish state that mixes dreams in giant swirls with my square-one condition, pooled in the lower back corner of the rumbling automobile. At one point, Chrissa looks back to find me like a whacked-out snake trying to get comfortable in the darker cavity of the floor behind the front seat.

And I can't *breathe*. I suddenly realize my breath is shallow, that I can't capture that deep, whole, complete breath that founds any sense of peace, and I struggle repeatedly to catch one, and fail and feel like I am suffocating for a panicked instant and have to consciously grip myself and determine to ignore it.

I try not to think because thinking means only one thing: of heroin. I try to just endure, to wait, like a vegetable, but the poisons in my body make me curse and spit and gripe and then think. What else is there? Drink. Masturbation. To pass the time. Ugh.

Chrissa asks me how I'm doing and I just mumble something

curtly. My mouth has that awful gland-taste in it. A resolution will strike me and I'll be able to rise out of the stewing turmoil and it all seems trivial and self-inflicted, but still I can't speak very well. She asks if there is anything she can do to help and I'm only able to say no. When I move back up to the front seat I try to explain to her how it feels, but so much of it is wrapped up in whirling streams of opposing impulses I can't convey it. Every sentence suggests its opposite and they batter me and I can only search and stumble across bad stretches of silence. Half my brain just wants it to be over so bad. What do I have to hope for if it isn't the dope that will take all this away? Shut up.

I look at Chrissa. She is something I can hope for. Fuck that. I already have her. If she had to know me straight neither of us could stand it.

22

The country whizzes by as I inch in my slime, furious and bored. Hours, minutes, motel rooms, car, diners, bars, desert. All the idiots of America who aren't me. Chrissa. Things are as they were, I think to myself. I am in my framework, it makes me sick and I want to get high.

The heat is horrible. Simple heat. It is horrible. Who wants to be human like this? With underwear you have to pick away from yourself through your pants, a sticky surface to your skin that captures all the grimy grit—sheer physicality become a constant clumsy ordeal, like the twelve-year-old whose voice suddenly starts cracking, who suddenly has giant breasts, as if the human body doesn't belong in nature, it's an embarrassment, an anchor that's drowning you. I can't even get breathing right, and my dick is sore and raw which is really bad for my disposition.

It makes me realize what a luxury "love" is. It's for children. Once you grow up and see how your emotions are governed by biological functions and the dynamics of social power it becomes clear that if the word has any meaning at all it's as a decision or a weakness, or it's the name for a feeling that is really independent of its expression, its "object"—the thing that attaches to it . . . Chrissa will totally irritate me, I'll be indifferent to her, and then overflow with gratitude.

Sometimes I used to fantasize about founding a Junkie Pride movement. It would be great to have hundreds and thousands of marching addicts, heads held high, waving placards that read GOD NODS and BOOZE & TOBACCO = DRUNK AND DEAD/SMACK & OPIUM = GREAT IN BED, TV crews flagging down proud protesters for interviews along the parade route. Tall, bony punk in dark glasses taking a question, "Have I ever mugged anyone? What if

I asked you if you ever raped a white woman? Junkies aren't violent." Abashed young kid in jeans and sneakers adds, "Alcoholics are." Skinny little pale art critic lady with facial blemishes pipes in, "The only serious violence associated with narcotics is perpetrated by the mob importers who get rich because of this country's insane policy of prohibition. If the government would tax narcotics one hundred percent it would still be cheaper than the illegal drugs we're forced to use now and not only would the nation make a fortune, but you'd put a lot of gangsters out of business."

It hurts too much though, it hurts too much, it hurts too much.

The dope years are a rite of passage, I think. A time in the desert. A war. What are the lessons I learned? Everything you do you do to yourself and there is no blame. I need to stop railing at the world for my condition. Humans are weird hybrids distinguished by these overdeveloped intellects that incline them to imagine ideals way beyond the capacities of their otherwise simple animal nerve-circuits. Nothing changes in global human terms, except on an evolutionary scale way too gradual for anyone to see. . . . What was I thinking? Um, I'm losing my train of thought . . . What . . . ?

Fuck shit piss. This heat sucks. I'm so sick of no subject but dope, but withdrawal is ruining my perfect motel rooms. There's no one it bores more than me. I know, I know—it's between me and God and leave you out of it. Spare you. Sullen, sweatsheened, bad vibe for company . . .

We drive through Lovelock and Tuscarora, Riddle, Magic City, Pocatello, Portage, Honeyville, Corinne, and Bountiful . . . All day it's "Thank you" and "I'm sorry" to Chrissa, but her patience hardly ever wears through. After a few nights when it gets to where my dick has largely healed and me and my horse flies can bear to touch the skin of another, I lie with my arms around her swearing to myself to remember . . . bathed clean and suspended in the peace and animal warmth she has miraculously become unrestricted to me, and I pull her around and kiss her and it is so tender and safe the sex feels like discovery, like coming together upon unexpected gifts that each of us want not for ourselves but to offer the other, and again I think this must be what love is, however ephemeral, it doesn't matter, to know it once is to know it finally, and it's simply essential to it and right and inseparable that it's not permanent and exclusive. Other men will take her there, other women me—so what, we love each other and all the questions and speculations are dust and ashes.

I don't worry about the book and she allows that.

One night we stop near a huge lake. After midnight we go out for a walk down to its shore. There are no streetlights and the sky is cloud-filled. A half moon comes clear two or three times, low in the sky, and then slides in dully lighted films of atmosphere back beneath, like something in the bottom of a drawer. Only it is us who are under. We pass the well-kept little trailer park opposite a cinder-block bingo parlor along the dark and silent road that leads to the lake between swelling smells of vegetation, insects buzzing, and the sudden clunk and flutter of roused water birds. At the edge of the water is a narrow rim of sand with a few metal and plastic chairs strewn near the scrub grass. We sit on the perfunctory beach with our knees to our chests. The air is thick with moisture but cool and fragrant, and we can just make out three empty small boats heightened by their reflections off in the invisible water before us. There are no stars. If you concentrate you can see different qualities of darkness meeting at the horizon but it seems like an illusion, like a clinging to the preconceived despite reality. The empty boats in fact are perfectly suspended in undifferentiated and indifferent enormity stretching to all sides. I want to be like that, I want to do something like that. I want to represent it. It is something worth praying to. I feel fed by it. It makes me happy. It's a happiness independent of narcotics.

I am still hard to get along with. I'm not giving much to Chrissa and I keep doing and saying petty little selfish things that I regret.

I don't know who I am here and I don't know how things are managed. I feel like Rip Van Winkle. I'm afraid and insecure and uncertain in everything, and don't know how to behave. I just want to be left alone but I don't know what to do with myself. I've forgotten how to feed and groom myself and every chore of daily life seems overwhelming. I don't like having a body and I hate being visible. My image of myself is of a furiously swiveling head catching the unsuspecting peripheral world in its act and lashing at it with mind rays, teeth bared and spitting with my eyes, a visage that paralyzes, burns, and shrivels whatever it beholds, but I don't have the energy for violence and in reality I am nothing but depleted, a meek being, nasty with impatience, ineffectual, whining, and resistant to the spending of any effort at all.

Chrissa gets some of her pictures developed and 8 x 10 prints made. She shows them to me. Most of them are in color. Every picture is of an idiot savant and every place is familiar and lost and forgotten and they are very pretty. I am amazed. How did she get that emptiness with just its smattering of perfect native morons? I can't believe it. The pictures are impossible. And there are these bright geometrical shapes hanging in the air of some of them. Where did that come from? The photos are truly great.

There is this one of a patchy-haired underfed young mutant with a weak lower jaw that is nevertheless too heavy for him to keep closed and skin like thin toothpaste that has little red specks on it and you can see the dirt in the lines of his neck and he is dressed in this exquisite Chinese dressing gown and sitting hunched over on a big sleek armchair in the foreground of a huge multileveled living room replete with antique chandelier, endless carpeting, impressionist and modernist paintings, full-length drapes that glow like radium, and sumptuously upholstered furniture scattered like rocks in a Japanese garden. The colors and composition are exquisite. He's holding a beautiful acoustic guitar as if he's playing for himself and the expression on his face is thoughtful and intelligent despite his obvious deprivation in those respects. By whatever means the shot was gotten, it is not fake—she has found something in its lair and captured it. The picture looks candid and it is beautiful and interesting as such and then your mind does a double take and it becomes even more interesting, chillingly, and you start thinking about it until your eyes take over again for simple pleasure and it is scary and great. You can't tell if he is totally witless or a very smart murderer.

Another has this big fat lady shot from behind bending over a little in the middle distance in her short thin print dress out of which her legs drop like massive dimply puffs of slop. It looks as if she's doing something there on the other side of the angle but you can't tell what. This is an exterior, apparently a GM car lot, big cars, and to the upper right of the frame is most of a little red triangle, out of nowhere. It looks like maybe she's farted it. Or is it a UFO? It doesn't seem to be drawn on there. It has some mass. The edge of something someone is carrying into the frame? What is the lady doing? It seems like a hot late afternoon but nobody is in sight except for a figure way off in the distance walking along the boulevard. You can see a couple of palm trees. The cars are gigantic. The picture is glossy and super-rich in color again and it looks sad but tough.

I am ecstatic. I look up at Chrissa like she's just grown wings or something. My mind is racing. She's carefully dealt me out five or six of them and I can see she's pretty sure about what she's done but she is also hanging on my reaction. "They're absolutely great and amazing," I say. "How'm I going to match them? Chrissa, you blow my mind. Wow." She looks like a complimented child, tentative, as if it could be taken away, but glad and proud. "I swear," I say, "they're like some kind of lifesaver thrown to me, or like a rope saving me from a fall at the last minute or something. What a team. I can tell, I can tell how great this book is going to be. They give me something to live up to and they're going to get me going so I can do it. Chrissa, you're a fucking genius. How'd you do this? I'm not going to ask. I'm not going to ask. Maybe you'll tell me some time, but it doesn't matter. You've done it. This book is going to be great. I'm totally turned on."

We wander around Nevada and Utah and the far south of Idaho for half a week and the days flatten out. I drink a lot. I don't know what else to do with my useless mind. I still can't sleep much.

I keep asking to see Chrissa's pictures until finally she lets me carry them. At night I look at her photos. From their strange completeness, their complete strangeness, I'm able to hook onto this passing sense of serenity and strength, a confidence that there is something worth doing that I can do. Then the hooks and wires slip and I feel like a leaning fence post, vaguely bewildered to be so pointless and witless. Then I look some more and I'm shored up again.

I am not responding to anything in the outside world. The landscapes are spectacular and the motel rooms my meat, but I have no appetite for them. I try to think about what it means to live in this country, what this country is, but it all seems obvious and boring. I mean, it is. What makes America America? Power and wealth won by cheating the naïve with irresistible promises of empty rewards. Arrogance. Do I have that correct? Ho hum. At the same time it is so big and handsome and out west it still feels as if nature's laws prevail rather than man's and there are still good places to get lost.

But where does that leave me? In the condition I am in, it is clear that the fundamental effect of heroin has been to relieve anxiety and kill time. Without it I have no identity, I am nothing but complaining nerves. I can't *do* anything. I need to do something in order to get a reflection of myself to know I exist, but I can't do anything. If my purpose isn't to get high, what can it be? Could it be to write? Am I a writer? No, that is another pose, another kind of game to play to pass the time. Stop thinking, stop thinking, stop thinking.

It is ironic, too—this desperate lunging for some mental tent pole—and my self-doubt feels like some kind of karmic payback for hubris, some kind of cosmic "How do you like it *now*?" for the smart-ass intellectual constructs I'd airily put forth over the years, arguing against the value and meaning of identity. From the safety of heroin I took my fear of my own emptiness and formlessness and tried to transform it with affirmation into a virtue. This gave me permission to do whatever I felt like as a man and an artist. I sneered that the idea of "finding" oneself was a coward's search for security and that it was more true and interesting to accept and indulge every contradictory whim and impulse, that we are much larger than we allowed ourselves to be and it is only our fearful and petty capitulation to the demands of the marketplace that constrain us. It is more exciting and true to interior reality to live on the edge of one's being, always capable of going in any direction without fear that it's inconsistent with some self-concept or established image.

Now, without dope, that seems like a disgusting lie, an inherently self-contradictory embroidery, that I had the luxury of fashioning in the leisure of heroin. Heroin gave me the cushion of removal from my own healthy fear to make such an idea embraceable. Now it feels treacherous, like a film noir femme fatale, chillingly, fatally dangerous, way beyond my inner means and drive, and in fact a self-serving attempt to put a good face on my own ugly weakness of character. What I'd really been addressing, attempting to cope with or disguise, was an ennui, a locked-in and timid paralysis, a scared need to be all things to all people, an anxiety in the face of decision, that was all negative, intrinsically ugly and pathetic, whatever it's named. That's how it seems now, that's how it feels as I am withdrawing. I am going out of my mind, but not far enough: I know that my impulse to intellectually arrange everything to put myself in the best possible light is ultimately, in the deepest privacy, between me and God, self-defeating. That "thought" is a realm of its own, castles in the air, and that what I need is to stop thinking so much in order to integrate myself, that thought is only really a reflection of one's spiritual condition: You can't think yourself into paradise, health, serenity. Thought follows experience, being, not the other way around.

Sometimes I ask Chrissa who I am. It becomes another standing joke. Under a tree I ask her who I am and she tells me that my father died when I was a young boy and I've been confused ever since but have made great and beautiful art from the confusion, or that I am two eggs over easy with bacon, home fries, whole wheat toast, and coffee, or that I am a junkie struggling not to use, or that I'm a drunk and a fool, or that I am her traveling companion and collaborator, or that I am a tall, skinny Amer-

23

Now that I've seen Chrissa's pictures, my note-taking changes some. I still keep desultory track of what we do and see on the trip but I also start thinking about and fooling with what kind of text would go with them.

I look at the pictures and go into a kind of trance imagining the ideal book they'd inhabit. This doesn't lead very far, but it's exciting. The one thing that's clear is that the words that go with these pictures can't be any kind of story that uses them illustration style. Then again, I wonder what story I might be able to come up with that *would* be aptly illustrated by them. I think about that for a while. I know I don't want to cop out with some kind of easy, obscure, highbrow artiness. I want the book to be as extreme and complicated and messy as the worlds in this trip, and that Chrissa's pictures intimate. At the same time when I see the book in my head it is completely unconventional and uncompromising—it's like a Gypsy crystal ball that is carved from Kryptonite or something, containing a possibly dangerous conception of human life here that is molded in materials, from points of view, that are fresh because alien-intelligent, that operates from different assumptions, namely mine, ours.

Immediately I have another idea, wondering what will happen if I imagine each picture as taken from someone's private photo album, as if each of the people in the pictures is known to someone else who keeps a secret photojournal where he or she scribbles innermost arias to the tunes of the snapshots. For instance a convict ruminating hotly as he masturbates to the accompaniment of the picture of the fat lady in the car lot, remembering how she'd fart these little red triangles as he'd fuck her doggy-style . . .

America feels boring. I feel sociopathic, smooth on the outside, violently cut off within. This is the reflection of America. How are you supposed to spend your damned life? What is there to aspire to? Fame and money. Sex and drugs. What else is there to do with freedom? Well, that's kind of interesting. And the overwhelmingness of the experience of the possibilities leads to that whole American rack tearing our left sides toward religion and our right to murder.

We stop in Salt Lake City.

Sometimes we wonder if the whole country is a collection of cults. Salt Lake City, beautiful name, and so welcoming. Everybody is smiling again, everything is clean. We have the best breakfast of the trip and my favorite hotel. The hot, wide streets are lined with beautifully maintained buildings from the twenties and earlier. The mania for the new seems absent.

Our famous breakfast is served in a big, airy, fifty-year-old art deco cheap lunchroom with fantastic lighting fixtures at the booths that balance iridescent, reflective globes on angled, grooved struts pushing out from the wall. I have a whole fresh trout with thick slabs of bacon and homemade hash browns, plus coffee with heavy cream, for $3.50.

Our hotel is in the poorest part of town and is an old-fashioned three-story warehouse of rooms with a lobby the size of a sound stage filled with big overstuffed furniture. The only occupants appear to be quiet old men, a few of whom are off toward its perimeters in their armchairs watching a TV set up on a coffee table. Ceiling fans turn reassuringly in the good soft light. The stairways and halls are as wide as streets and they are not only clean but freshly painted. A double room is $19 a night.

We can't find any bars and it's embarrassing to have to ask. Mormons don't approve of alcohol. When we finally find one it is strange. It's a typical dark little streetfront saloon with a small neon sign and country music on the jukebox but it's too quiet and there's an unmistakable sense of shame inside the place. The few people inside seem beaten and defensive about being there. One guy is a middle-aged American Indian and he seems especially ashamed. It's in the air in the room. The drinkers give off a sense of hopeless failure, as if this is clearly the last stop for the worst losers. There's no feeling of fun or even defiance or mutual support of any kind among them. They are even ashamed to be seen by one another.

We leave the bar and go to a movie. *Urban Cowboy* is playing. Classic Hollywood star vehicle melodrama, perfect for Salt Lake City, and if I were high I could fall into it happily, but I'm too antsy, squirming in my seat, having to resist wishing it were over because really there'll be even less to do then.

I am bored. I don't want to try and make something of all this. I just want to get high. Out of this awful skin. That night I call New York and persuade a couple of friends to overnight me a package containing ten dimes of dope to General Delivery in Denver.

24

I don't tell Chrissa. I hardly even tell myself. I act as if everything is the same. When the subject of my continuing abstinence arises, I just pass over it, grunting assent as if I'm in a mood and I don't have the patience to talk about it. I'm used to disappointing expectations. It's comfortable, almost pleasant.

I have 36 hours to kill before that dope will be in Denver. I wait through the night in the hotel racking up a surprising five-plus hours of sleep, and then the next day I tell Chrissa I don't feel up to exploring and she goes off alone while I stay in the room.

I'm reading a true-crime paperback about a serial killer. I get scared by how thoroughly I identify with him. He's an intelligent, personable guy who wanders the country in his little automobile regularly making dates with girls whom he murders. Then he sexually explores their corpses. It's uncanny how intimately I can feel his inner processes. They begin with his sense of aloneness and apartness, a failure to understand why anyone does anything, and it's a way of being in the world that runs so deep that he's long past, at some blurry corner in his childhood, accepted it irrevocably so that it's his nature. He's found he has a talent for gaining people's confidence and that these people, women really—they are the only people he gives time to—take him at face value and only he knows that the face is false, that there is no face, no face at all to his being, but even he doesn't know it anymore: He is simply behaving like everyone else.

I don't want to dramatize myself. There is something too chic and self-absorbed and repulsively self-congratulatory in claiming to identify with a serial killer, but still I feel like I know him so well, from the inside. How that first time some girl made him do it, how he lost it and his fury was unleashed, how he help-lessly lost patience with the way she keeps demanding all this ridiculous behavior from him before she'd let him have sex with her, while she giggles coyly and playacts herself, fuck her, give her a taste of the real underneath, all the huge implacable underneath and see how she likes it instead of swishing around and putting me through hoops, the fucking idiot, the little shit fool, you're making me do it and that's a surprise that wakes you up, for the last time, as you die. And he kills her off in the woods where they've parked in his little foreign car.

And he never even hears himself think these things, he is taken over by the force of his final separateness, his utter absence of empathy. And then he has the taboo naked body all to himself. He's never even thought of that and there it is, all that sex package to make you swoon and your throat to choke with the moment of what could be done.

The first time is a surprise. It just happens. But it gives him something to do, and as scared of being found out as he is after-ward, no one ever even comes and knocks on his door about it. "Life" goes on as if nothing had happened. And there it is, stew-ing in the back of his mind, hot in a glade there, like a new evo-lutionary feature developed, as if he is Clark Kent and only he knows the amazing secret power that sets him apart and he walks among men appearing ordinary.

I know why he does it again and again after the first time. There are two reasons. The first is that once he has done it at all his virginity is gone and the restraints are broken. The world didn't collapse when he broke the taboo and the thrill was so great and the act so extreme that it becomes who he is. It has to be kept fresh. Once its immediacy starts to fade it's only a bur-den, but with every new murder and sex act it is ecstacy, an arrival at the real again. The second is that he wants to get caught. Part of the source of the power of the act is his defiance of everything. He is baiting the world, the universe, and he baits it more and more viciously with every killing, if in no other way than by sheer repetition. And baiting is meaningless unless the bait's eventually taken.

As I read his story, intuiting his state of mind, I feel sick and depressed, ghastly. It actually changes the flavor of the hours. I feel as if I've been found out—finding myself out again, under that rock—and it is a gooshey, vertiginous, queasy feeling. I feel constantly on the verge of tears. This is too much.

I am so glad the dope is coming, but that feeling, too, concealed from Chrissa, contributes to my weaselly, beaten-dog state. I feel like hitting myself, low wash of trancey thrill in the notion of taking my fists and crunching the bones of my face. But, as with Merry, this gets suppressed till all that is outwardly detectable is a continuous low-level irritation, a bad mood.

I go outside and it seems my heart will break. The town looks so good and the outside so big and open with all its little entrances and it is unavailable to me. In 24 more hours I'll be high. Everything else is waiting time. I am an addict again.

When Chrissa gets back I tell her I want to get moving because I sleep better in the car. In fact I know it will be a two-day drive to Denver so I want to get at least halfway today.

We drive for eight hours and stop at a motel just a hundred and fifty miles from Denver. I tell her I'd like to get an early start in the morning. The night isn't too bad except for the few times it happens that I realize I've been clean for a week and the rush of exhilaration will be followed by a terrible shame, but this gets ground down to a single-minded, tight, and bitter determination focused on the wait until I get my drugs.

Once we are out of town in the morning and on our way, I tell her what I've done. I am totally tired and shut off but I try to explain to her how I am beaten, I'm just beaten and I've done the only thing I know to do. I tell her I am sorry but I am what I am and as little as I might like it there is nothing else to say but that it is my nature. I tell her that I am just scared, just scared, I'm not going to lie, to pretend that I am choosing, I'm not choosing, I've lost. I've lost and I can't even stand to think about it. Anymore. I just want to get the dope.

Chrissa doesn't get angry and she doesn't take what I say personally. She isn't disgusted with me. She says something that shakes the inside of my head in this tiny way that I don't even notice at first but has a kaleidoscopic kind of effect, a little tremor that produces a shift that seems actually dramatic. She says that what she can't stand about my drug use is the way it makes me hate myself. This moves me, as usual, at her beauty and unselfishness, but also at the uncomplicated truth of it which somehow I'd never seen in exactly that way, with such simplicity. In the past I would have thought, no it's the other way around, I take the drugs because I hate myself or I hate the world but *boiiing,* her words, it's the same thing, yes; I'm killing the world/myself in the act of using them and is that what I really want to do? It rearranged things in this little tiny way that is important. Something starts to crystalize. It changes the light and it seems things won't ever look exactly the same now.

25

All the way to Denver I feel like a very old man. There isn't any pleasure in going to pick up the dope, there is just habit and weariness. I have to focus, cut off my peripheral perception from all the fluttering fears and doubts and arguments, and concentrate on the security of routine, like an athlete, or a soldier.

I tell Chrissa that, that I feel like a marathon runner, steeling myself, taking one minute at a time, pushing single-mindedly toward the goal, batting away all doubts, heroically, stoically ignoring the temptation to simply stop running. It's funny. Going to cop is a lot like not going to cop. She asks why I don't just bypass the post office and I tell her it's too late. Habit.

By the time we get to Denver the package has arrived and I pick it up without a hitch. I drive from the post office, a big new building on the edge of town, to the first gas station, buy a soda pop, lock myself in the men's room, cook up in the bottle cap with a piece of cigarette filter for cotton, and get off. I get back in the car and we drive on.

The drug does what it always does. Gives me a big kiss and takes me in its arms and holds me and gives me all aid and comfort, says welcome back, you look great and everything's OK now we're together again. And what does it want in return? Ten, twenty, sixty, eighty bucks a day and whatever other efforts it takes to search out and acquire itself, and then every second of my time.

I take over driving. We've come out of the dramatic mountains and are rolling across high gray-green hills where cattle graze, the Rockies in the distance.

I am at ease and lubricated again and I talk to Chrissa. I tell her how real Americans are drug addicts. It is the "pursuit of happiness," it is capitalism, it is freedom, it is individualism in wide open spaces, it is democracy. It is DeSoto Adventure. I don't know what the fuck all I say, and she lets me go on, waltzing with me in the chatter, and then I catch myself feeling I am putting something over on her and I hate that.

I get this sense of myself as a child who's hoodwinked an adult, who's gotten an adult to give in against knowledge and judgment to some stupid stubborn wish, like for another cotton candy, and the way the child gets all expansive and loquacious and self-assured like some pompous bureaucrat in its ego-flush, carefully restraining the urge to gloatingly laugh and sneer at its pitiful victim but all self-satisfied . . .

It's humiliating. I am in this position that eliminates the possibility of having any pride. I can't pretend any longer that I want to do dope, but here I am doing it, so where am I? Who's I? How can I explain it? What I is here to do the explaining?

Some kind of balance has shifted. The dope has the same painkilling effect as always, but somehow, underneath, it feels like cowardice, like running home to mama cuz something gave me a dirty look. I can't hide though, there is no shelter from the shame, the loss of self-respect, the self-hatred. It comes with me, even into the euphoria, and I just have to try and manage to avoid where it is kept. I tell her these things, too, because I want someone to know, and describing it eases it, and she seems interested.

Chrissa wants to see New Mexico so we are driving south and despite all I get to doing pretty well at enjoying my high. After a while I'm too drowsy and I return the wheel to her. My head against the window, eyelids drooping, the goopy tides of pleasure take me and I nod and nap for hours.

When I wake up we are back in dense, piney mountains, a little smaller scale than in Colorado, on a twisting two-lane road. Chrissa says we've been in New Mexico for an hour, approaching Taos.

I take over driving again and I do everything I can to buy into the opportunities for peace of mind promised by the dope.

The trees thin out as we twist down out of the steep hills into the desert. Behind the wheel on the narrow back roads we take through the wildness I am in love again. I want to kiss everything, I want to eat the light, I want to inhale it all, everything I see, through my nose and eyes and ears and mouth. The barren land with its occasional weather-beaten roadside stops—diners and junk shops and half-assed Indian trading posts—isolated, dug-in, conforming to the immense indifference, corresponds perfectly to my inner state and makes me happy.

Chrissa over by the window in the big front seat lights me up. I feel lucky and I feel manly and I get the idea of fucking her in the desert. I want to fuck her cleanly and thoroughly and I have the feeling she wants to be fucked. She's been mothering me for days and giving me all the benefit of the doubts and now for a while the doubts are swept under the rug—it's a vacation, home from work, time off, a reprieve. I am all outward confidence and tenderness and she is glad for the break from nursing, glad to give up the responsibilities of caretaking, and all the coyness is gone between us and I know that the drug will let me fuck for hours and nothing would please me more than to take her where everyone wants to go, and just fuck and fuck.

The swells of lightheaded, big-dicked impulse surge in spells and build, until late in the afternoon it comes to a head and I pull over and stop beside a little desert road. In this act it is hardly even personal, or it is metapersonal, it is a man and a woman. The mannish man feels like fucking a woman and the womanly woman feels like being fucked by a man and they both know it and that's all there is to it. Carrying an Indian blanket I'd picked up in a junk shop, I lead her across a roadside stream by its tattered screen of trees and we walk into the desert until we feel sufficiently engulfed in it and distant from the car and the dead-quiet road, like it's a kind of darkness, and I fuck her brains out. Nothing has ever felt so sexy. It does matter of course that it is her, Chrissa, who has her will and her self-possession and her varying stances regarding me and whom I thirst for and whose response to me has always mattered. Chrissa, that face and proud naked body become purely given up to my ragingly hard dick on the grainy, hard-packed desert floor. And she wants me to feel that power, even anger, blood lust, conquering drive, fuckly aggression, she doesn't care, she laughs in the middle of it with delight to allow it done upon her, to get its benefits, and ride it and embrace it and the ultra-intense abandon that doesn't exclude skill and strategy. It is her giving over of herself that makes her pleasure possible because it is rare and scary, dangerous to her and exciting to me and it is my excitement that makes the whole thing possible, because that is how dicks get hard and we both laugh. And it doesn't let up and she just gets wetter and wetter and more and more astonished and her cheekbones burn red and she hacks and screams in orgasms, and I slow for a minute and then it reaches the top again and then goes over it. I look down at my cock coming in and out of her and that seems anonymous and I want it to be her and I tell her *It is me, it's Billy,* and she opens her eyes and her glassy-eyed glazed face gets this feral watchful triumphant look like a cat about to pounce and she says *I'm Chrissa and you're fucking me out of my mind* and her eyes close and her face goes beatific and spaced again and the rhythm changes a little bit, rising, and we both laugh from all the way inside, hoarsely, and in a second she comes some more. I don't have it let up. There comes a point after two or three series of her orgasms where she makes as if to have me stop but I resist and jam her through once more to where you really can't tell if she is being killed and her cunt is erupting all around my cock and it's like she is getting electroshock and noises like farts and spurts of mucous are splashing up into my pubic hair and it is just as it should be, everything all broken down and dissolved and shattered and exhausted and I lie on her, my dick still hard as a rock inside that gulping melted slush, throbbing till it settles like we sink to the bottom and rest there, nestling beneath it all.

When I pull out and slide to the side, oblivious to the grating smudging dirt, and wrap my arm and knee across her, head bowed to hers, she whimpers tinily because she's liked enclosing me in that resting place. In a little while we get up and get dressed like coal miners or oil field roughnecks at the end of the

26

I know someone a little in Santa Fe, a writer whom I haven't seen for years and years, since I first came to New York, but his name is in the phone book and I call him up. He invites us to come stay with him and his wife, but I don't want to do that—I like our motels. I don't want to have lunch at his house the next day either, where we'll be stuck in his territory without being able to leave quickly enough if I want to. So we agree to meet the two of them at a restaurant.

Santa Fe is a dusty little Spanish and Indian town that white people have made self-important. It is the worst kind of bad art ghetto. I cringe to be here. It is good for my junkiness though. It makes me proud to be an addict. My habit is an automatic and continuous current of protest against and rejection of the place. I like being a bruise of freelance disgust on its smug self-satisfaction. These white people think they own the beauty of the place when in fact they are the stain on it, their ecological consciousness and all. And I am the stain on them. The dumb fucks.

I was here before for a couple of months when I was 18 and sure enough, it remains the same. Wide quiet small-town streets between scattered cubes in adobe and tile, cottonwood trees for plenty of shade, earthen and compact among low hills of soft desert scrub in the crisp and fragrant air, mountains in the distance. Then like sutures, like giveaway tucks of plastic surgery, there are the art galleries, the pretentious little restaurants, the shiny four-wheel-drive vehicles. Somewhere here, unvisible to the fat invaders, it is certain there are those with lives that partake of the real forces of the underlying landscape. The land is so strong that it has to be that it feeds some fundamental and circumspect human souls organic to it, despite all the corrupt and arrogant impositions, and they will recognize one another and they comprise the human integrity of the place, but that isn't my territory either.

We meet this big grinning guy with his sparkly eyes and prom-queen-gone-natural of a wife the next morning about noon. I want to steal something from him. The infuriating thing is that Chrissa can't seem to see it, how revolting they are. He thinks he is some kind of macho handyman, some kind of Dad kind of writer, in charge of what to do next, with all the hidden resources of dick that takes. Well, fuck him. Let him die in it. It'll catch up with him. I'm not gonna waste my time.

I'm pissed at Chrissa though. How can she tolerate this shit? These French are so fucking civilized and they like going around and having affairs too. He wants to talk to me about punk, as if it is privileged and by knowing me he's in on it, while at the same time he's condescending. I have no better response than to get rude and treat him like a dumb journalist. I keep saying things like "it wasn't" and "no" that stop the conversation and I start ridiculous, lying anecdotes plausibly, just to lead him on and make him out a fool. I'm a brat and it gets ugly and we are lucky to get out of there without it all breaking open and him causing me physical damage.

Driving back to the motel it occurs to me again that I'm not learning very much. I'm not seeing anything I don't know, and this particular stop is a regression. I ask Chrissa if she'd like to take a picture of my asshole. That is something I don't think a rock star has done yet. I could get out of the racket with a flourish. "No thanks," she says. "Well, maybe if you really want me to." No, I say, never mind.

I can't get fucking high enough to find my steady relief. I can feel these shitty feelings nagging at me from below, pushing through again, no matter how stoned I get myself. I don't even name them in hopes that that will keep them at bay. I want it to be OK to get high—I keep turning up the drug volume to drown them out but the nagging voices are coming from inside and I can't seem to escape from them. How pedestrian, I think, trying to parry, deflate, undermine, conquer the noises: how common-place, bourgeois . . .

Things aren't right. Where the fuck do I go from here? Back to the motel and more drugs and sex? Maybe I could degrade Chrissa. Suck her into something uglier than she's ever thought possible and we could revel in it like screaming faces. Come up against the purposelessness of scrabbling down in the muck and slinging the slime around, to where you realize you've done it to nothing but yourself and you're alone with it, and you get that fabulous heart-gone feeling. But I know that already and how many times can you crack your own innocence? Pretty often. It'd fill some time with good old-fashioned heartbreak, it'd be real.

But in fact I'm not really even up to it. I don't have what it takes. I don't want to hurt anybody, even myself, and Chrissa is way ahead of me anyway. I am scared and I am phony, I have no direction left. I can just drive. I am ready to drive. Driving is great. America *is* big. That's one thing about it. It makes the days different from one another.

The car is acting kind of funny. Sometimes as we get up over sixty it will stop accelerating for a moment, there'll be a little clunk in the push before it catches again. It isn't hampering us badly, though, and there is no scary sound or smell and it doesn't seem to be getting worse, so we just keep on, figuring the engine is old—it's bound to have some quirks. I do think Chrissa is pushing it too hard. We try a couple of things gas station attendants suggest but they don't make much difference.

We push up through corners of Texas and Oklahoma into Kansas on our way to Kansas City. Kansas is pretty boring— another part of the heartland that is famous for its murderers and other simple people. But I have no real initiative to investigate. I am only going through the motions, looking out at things from this slow, dopey, soft little place in myself. It has been a long long time since I've learned anything from dope. It is like jerking off and going to sleep. Continuously, in and out of the days, like an idiot, a monkey, a monkey in a laboratory. Meanwhile it removes me from the immediate. My mind is elsewhere and I cannot be trusted by anyone including myself. I twist within this knowledge, everything ruined.

Chrissa is sick of it. It gets bad in the car. I have no basis. It's like we'd once been together and now she's been pulled away from me and the better part of me got torn off with her. I want to be her. I am drawn to her, but to her I am just a parasite.

And as we drive along the road, the road splays like fiber and each strand of tar-joined gravel curls back and rays outward, crumbling toward us from their farthest reaches like fuses into the enormous reaches of nothingness at their tips that separates the system of atomic particles in the haze ahead of us as we drive.

I lose my reality to myself in the worst way. This is what makes me know I am a false person and a loser and a freak whose very existence is an embarrassment. The French I think have no geek class—they read the quality of geekness as charming and respectable—so Chrissa is more angry than contemptuous, but I know. I want to spread out and be crucified and go wheeling off into the dead but I am too shy. I don't have the substance. My wits are dim and warped, refracted from misconnections in my mind, and I stutter, misunderstanding. God speaks to me and I get all huffy, saying I don't have to take this and I walk out, the wrong door, and God calls a warning and I turn and call back inappropriately offended, and then I slip—*oops*—and get up and keep walking, the other way, muttering to myself, in my ridiculous clothes . . . I never even know what is happening. I am one of those. Shouldn't I die to make it real? I was saying lemme out of here before I was even born.

I have this realization that all my conscious life I've treated myself as a given thing incommensurate with the world and I've tried by the framing of myself in relation to it—my clothes, my friends, that which I profess, my self-description, mood-changing substances—to find some placement, to thread myself in if even by protesting, and it is impossible. It occurs to me that I've gone about it backwards—there is no way that I can remake the world, even only the bubble of aura surround me, so that it corrects by corresponding to my childish fear and yearning for comfort and dominion, the will of the world would not be remade even in its smallest part by any being, but already by virtue of birth I am a vein and current of it and all and the only thing to do is to be that with some kind of humility and gratitude. The world itself is interesting, much more interesting than I who am merely one miniscule capillary in and of it. We think it's glamorous to assert ourselves when in fact it's only foolish and sad and obviously futile. (But this is a judgment too, which I have no right to make . . .)

27

Then again, what the hell? Here I am. I can see my hands and arms. I have a history. I am rolling, bankrolled, in a '57 DeSoto through the wheat fields and cattle farms of Kansas toward Kansas City, blood loaded with the best care-reliever money can buy. I'm just a man and all I really know is what my blood tells me. I love my mistakes. Fuck it.

We stop at a motel on the outskirts of a tiny town on the plains. Chrissa takes the car and camera to look around.

I pull out her pictures and look at them. I think a good way to gain the upper hand again would be to get together a sample text to show her.

It's hard. I stare and stare at the pictures trying to think of how any words can augment or complement them.

I think of this crazy guy I once knew and how he'd radically and how radically he would bend all his experience to fit into the strange world inside his head. He interpreted anything that happened, the most ordinary occurrences, in these haywire personal terms. He would see a crossing guard at an intersection as a member of a secret society pressing certain philosophical points into the minds of school children, or unfamiliar toppings on pies behind the counter of a pizzeria as pancreas of goat and stingray skin. But no matter what tone or point of view I imagine for a text to go with the pictures it always feels extraneous. The pictures are pure and their mystery rebuffs any elaboration.

I think of trying captions like tabloid headlines, such as "Heir Spends Millions on Face-lifts for His Penis," or simple platitudinous truths like, say, "Fear is Lack of Faith." I think of using the photos somehow so they physically mottle and shadow the text, making the words like mysterious clues. That gives me a strange moment of feeling myself to be an inhabitant of the photo world, as if I am the product of someone else's mind and I can no more see them than I can myself.

How can pictures and words do more than illustrate each other? It seems like the only other possibility is high and complicated art that incorporates words that work as directly as pictures do, and I don't know where I'd begin and it's too far from our assignment. Then I think of just writing personal emotional true-life facts around the pictures, and I start:

[When it occurs to me, when I remember, when it's convenient] At the moments that such a thing is imaginable [when I'm not distracted, when I don't forget] I'm [totally, "romantically"] in love [my girlfriend, my lover] with her [Chrissa, the person who took these pictures]. [Moments . . . movements . . . bowel movements.] I'm frightened of her because she has power over me. I thank her and I apologize to her as if she were God. I'm her dog. I have faith in her. At the time she was taking these pictures she was disgusted and angry with me because I'd been flirting with the desk clerk at our motel. I'm sure she forgot all about me as she was making the pictures. I was fucking the desk clerk and my dick was really big and hard and the whole thing was perfectly spectacular, like a good shit. A little later Chrissa went to the length of secretly smelling my underwear to find out what I'd done. When she tried to kill me I kissed her, but it wasn't me and it wasn't her, it was entirely a kiss. All this kind of thing makes your heart hurt and you feel crazy. [shit motif here]

Chrissa took these two pictures in L.A. I was doing what she is going to do tomorrow: fuck someone else. Los Angeles: where the highways [freeways] gather to feed, the landscape folds and snaps back like an abused animal. Where America hits the wall and bounces off, trying to smile, stars popping in its head [around its brain]. These curly hills entirely unsuited for human habitation. Taste it. It wants to give it to you. Nobody'll know and you can even call it something else. But gee, I feel so sad. Sadness is self-indulgence, incompetence, unadult, not allowed. You shouldn't tell a child it can do anything. That everything's allowed. How was I to know? Well, these things happen. Today is the first day of the rest of your life. It's not that things don't have consequences, but that you're going to die anyway so you might as well look at the money. It's spiritual. Help me.

Shit something along those lines might work. I don't see how you could make a movie out of it, and it would be a lot of work without being very widely appreciated, but I don't think Jack could really argue with it too strongly—I think he'd have to respect it—and even if it is angry and a little depressed it would be funny, too. After all, America isn't really a very pretty picture. At least it isn't to me, and that's what he's paying for. And where it's pretty, I'd admit it.

I stand up from the chair and walk around the room. Sometimes I wonder what Chrissa does out there and how she gets those pictures but I think it's just as well I don't know. She never volunteers anything about it.

I switch on the TV and there is a nature show playing on the educational channel. On screen is some plantlike animal on the floor of the ocean prettily waving its bulbous translucent-milky big cilia-fringed mouths. The vaguely familiar authoritative murmur of the narrator praises the creature in tones of awe and kindness. The animate particles of food it is capturing could have no idea what is happening to them. They are too small and blind to ever even guess at their killer's existence. If they could, they'd be scared shitless, but no better able to escape.

I open the entrance to the outside where a few cars and pickup trucks are nosed against the walkway before the long row of motel room doors. Across the little three-lane highway is more corn. I walk outside. There is absolutely nothing here that points to anything else. It is just something to pass through, a time hole, that holds only what you already have, boredom, as blandly depressing as a child's Saturday morning with no one around. I go into the parking lot and stand there. I turn to my left and walk to the edge of the motel and then over the knobby grass and into the cornfield. I walk through the rows for thirty yards and stretch out in the dirt. I think, Here I am and no one anywhere can see me and I don't have any other thoughts except an awareness that I don't have any other thoughts. In a minute I see some ants in the dirt and I play with them with a little twig.

I look up at the sky and the spare cloud formations are unlike any I can remember having seen before. They are little irregularly shaped swatches that look like a soft gray corduroy of thick meandering ridges on a smeary background of half-erased chalk marks spattered across the blue. I wonder how big they are and how close. There is no way to judge. The windblown stiff puffs of tree-stands in the distance seem somehow made in the same conceptual pattern. So do the stalks, and broad-veined and speckled, perfectly graceful leaves of the corn plants rising around me. I can't tell what size any of it is. That feels completely peaceful for a moment and I am consistent with and subside into it.

I get the feeling that I've been here before, that as a child I have had exactly this moment alone in an indistinguishable place and time in Kentucky, and had somehow been fully aware that it would recur here as an adult as it now is. I mentally greet myself and it feels good.

28

We get to Kansas City with the idea of staying overnight and having the car looked at. I like the town but everything is only half-present. I am made of something that can't penetrate into where things happen among people. There is some kind of powerful surface tension repelling me. I suppose I am just a big-city boy. I can't understand people who aren't as fucked up as me. If it isn't about drugs or sex or art I don't get it. Yawn. Double yawn.

> Excuse me—
> I think I'm going to fart.
> Thank you for paying
> me for saying that.

The primordial urge to punk. The chemical reaction when anger is added to *Thank you, I'm sorry.* A goddamned tree is enough to make you angry. Everything is provincial and boring. The only society of any interest and soul and integrity is the drunks and drug users and sex peddlers and other criminals. But what—I am going to be going from town to town hanging in low-life bars trying to gain the confidence of petty thieves and appealing to the sexual despair of drug-starved trollops? No, I might as well go fully local and drive the car directly into one of the trees. I best stay stunned in my motel room, plotting and forgetting, plotting and forgetting, and then remembering and begging. And discarding and rejecting and resolving and forgetting. Don't think. Don't think. Don't think.

I miss my serene green couch. I don't want to be seen by Chrissa. I am a creature that flourishes only in solitude. That is the only place where I can suicide, I mean subside, into my self-conception—exposure to other humans challenges it.

Kansas City is a big border town kind of place, border between North and South, East and West, Kansas and Missouri, black and white. Charlie Parker's hometown. It is sleepy and it cooks. There are great old-fashioned prize fight–type posters for blues and R & B singers nailed and pasted everywhere in the neighborhood where we stay. I rip a couple down for souvenirs. It is the city where our car is most appreciated—everybody comments on it. The town seems loose and knowing, a cool and funky place.

I go out in the afternoon, the evening, and late at night for a few drinks but mostly I stay in the motel room and read and write in my notebook. I play tapes, too. I've picked up this little cassette player and a couple of portable speakers to plug into it. It is great to have music again. I can't believe I've gone these two weeks without it. I get some Billie Holiday and Miles Davis and old rockabilly and Jimi Hendrix and Aretha and Dylan. I even find some Stooges and Howling Wolf. I sit in the bed with my books and notebook beside me and a bottle of whiskey on the night table and the cassette player set up playing on the bureau opposite. The music remakes me, filling the room with emotion. It makes me recall why I'd wanted to play and sing and write.

The power of the music—what it gives you and does to you, where it takes you—seems impossible, like sorcery or subatomic physics, considering its simplicity. It's like the sun; and then the moon. How does it do that? I guess it must have something to do with the way music comes to you, you don't need to go to it the way you do with words. Then it encompasses, more dimensional even than light, instantly, and not by force but sympathy. It changes everything. And songs: The series and combinations of notes and how they are played and the nature of the instrument producing them, those sounds, are direct emotion itself; unlikely as it seems that that could be, there's a pure correspondence, you could probably analyze it like a scientist, and something in the design is in fact mathematical, giving you purely abstract pleasure, too, and then that's all mixed with the possibilities of the message and purposes of the words, and the rhythm physically taking and compelling you, the whole mess shooting all around bruised and popping and breathing, threatening and begging, projected in miniscule waves that carom and vibrate so that you literally move inside it and are penetrated by it. And that doesn't even touch on the appeal of a given person's voice and how it is a friend or not, or a sex thing, or an oracle, smart, sweet, honest, or angry or tough—all the character that's carried in a voice exposed to where it gives you something you get nowhere but your most intimate intense relationships. It seems amazingly good of them to do this for us.

And it can be produced by one person holding a guitar. And you can have it all and all the different kinds for a few dollars worth of tape and a cassette player. Push a button and there it is. I stretch out in it, utterly given and grateful, sipping whiskey and looking at my books and now and then taking a pencil to a notebook in the motel in Kansas City, four bags of dope left.

It is like I have my cave back and I am transhuman in it. There is something great about being a stranger. And the music is the serum, the potion, the transformative elixir. It eases and brings me back into the world, where I belong. I listen and then I can walk out in the anonymous dusk and survey our quiet and beautiful estate, Kansas City: Big old oaks on dusty lawns of dignified architecture warped and peeling but serene, corner-turned from yea-high cement and wooden teeth of dark little bars, mismatched autorepair, and cheap motels the homes to pimps and whores, all tinged and linked to common stretching shadows from far beside the sidelong, ever-warm if distant faded rose and golden setting sun, pedestrians of courtesy. I know it is bloodthirsty but I'm not immediately threatened and the blood thirst is intrinsic and inseparable from its beauty anyway. All of it is ordinary.

Who's to say which soul of us is more or less worthy? No one. Not at all, nor in any respect.

29

It's one of the few times we're on an interstate, approaching St. Louis, when the car breaks down. Chrissa is driving and the accelerator just goes useless and she steers off onto the shoulder.

Immediately the car seems fake, like junk, and it reflects on us. Death is embarrassing. It's as if we've been fools to ever have acted as if it were ours and now we are being shown up. All its glow is gone and it's leaking onto the pavement.

Under the gigantic overcast sky by the side of the busy road we are very small but too conspicuous. Reflexively I blame Chrissa for the breakdown. She resents that, of course, but my next-to-last two bags are protecting me and I just sullenly let her share some of my haze of fuzzy anger. I have it to spare. It's a grey day, an ugly highway, the car is dead, and it's all interfering with my borderline nod. St. Louis, mundane as shit. Too damn close to the Northeast but totally New Yorkless.

We get ourselves towed to a gas station. In an hour the mechanic there says it's the transmission and will be a major repair.

We are about a day's drive from my hometown in Kentucky. I insist to Chrissa that we tow the car there to get it fixed. I have my heart set on visiting my near-forgotten hometown and I think I can probably get drugs in Lexington. I say that I know we can get a mechanic we can trust there and furthermore, that I don't want to be stuck for days in the wasteland 15 miles out of St. Louis. Chrissa accepts this.

I pretend I know what I'm doing and get on the phone to make arrangements. Amazingly, I manage. There is a U-Haul truck we can pick up tomorrow morning that'll tow the DeSoto. My aunt in Lexington not only has room to put us up but knows a good place we can deliver the car.

We check into a motel a few yards from the gas station. I want to start early so I'll get to Lexington in time to find some drugs while I'm still OK. I'll be doing my last bags in the morning. I feel stretched thin and tight. It always seems surprising and somehow illogical that a lot of something can run out. I have to scratch my head over it like some kind of x-eyed dimwit. There had been so much dope and I always just used part of it. How could it be gone? How come you always just had to start everything all over again? It doesn't make sense and it's confusing and it pisses me off.

I call my connection friends in New York again. It takes a colder and colder three hours to reach them but they finally answer. They got the money I sent them for the last batch and agree to do it once more to my aunt's address.

I wake up just before dawn and lie beneath the covers in the recurring dimness. I'm not sick, but I'm in that in-between condition where my mind is gaping and things are crawling around in it. I'm sharp and quick but I feel a million years old, like someone who will never die and that is his punishment. It isn't really unpleasant except that I'm aware of what the next stage will be, but that's all right because of the two bags nestled safely in a pants pocket in my clothes bag. I know I've returned to where I've let the drug cut all my ties and in a kind of distantly stunned and resigned way I don't just welcome but revel in it. I love it and it kind of makes me sick and the drug will take care of all that too.

I think of putting off using it and going outside and looking at the sunrise but then I say to hell with it, I have the sunrise tucked in my tiny paper sacks. I get up in my underpants and go and fish the bags out of the stack of folded clothes, get my belt and works and the bottlecap from my shaving kit, and take them into the bathroom and get off. Two bags still feel good and will hold me till tomorrow morning.

Damn, there's nothing like pleasure on demand. Why would I ever want to do without? I remember when I first did dope I'd thought, Wouldn't you know it? *The bastards*, they had to keep it for themselves—anything this good they have to keep for themselves. They treat us like children because they want us to be dependent on them. They think just because they're rich they're the only ones who deserve all the good things. The scumbags.

That was a long time ago. *Romantic music . . .*

I was so in love. Dope was so magic. We were Romeo and Juliet. It was just what I'd always wanted without even knowing it, stuff that lets you not only dream while awake, but gives you the power to prod and stroke and sculpt the dreams, introduce action and characters—to direct your own dreams. And dreams are just another form of being awake. With junk you can dream your life. And the flesh feels so good. The only little drawback is addiction and that's nothing—you have to do it every day for weeks to get a habit. That's no risk at all.

I go outside into the gray and smelly dawn. The air is damp. We are close enough to the interstate that I can hear the cars above the bird calls. The concrete and asphalt carways carved between the remaining small niches and graveyard plaques of stunted living woods, all threaded and arrayed with high sags of cable, give the impression that you are a bit of intruding grit, foreign matter, consciousness aside, in a machine too big to comprehend or even bother wondering about, except to resent its presumption. Clearly these things aren't put there like that for me, despite the jolly signs and billboards.

I turn around and go back into the room. I don't know what to do with myself. Chrissa is still asleep in the wide, fabric-softened darkness. I go into the bathroom and wash my face and brush my teeth. The only move I can think of taking is to get in bed with her.

I take off everything but my underpants and go and slide in under the covers beside her. I am facing along her back without actually touching her. I have my head on one forearm and the other elbow locked to my side. I feel gone and lost in the damp repeating room, awake as she sleeps, and wanting to hold her, to press my thick crotch into the smooth bulge of recourse muscle and fat that swells out from the small of her back and incidentally leads to her brain and feelings. It seems cold now that I am afraid, wanting things to be different than they are.

I lie there confused by her hair, baffled by her breathing, victim of some obscure and rending sense that lurks so far down in my emptiness and hollow that it practically fails altogether, but nevertheless dominates in the vacuum and identifies me, that my salvation lies in her. Basically there is just nothing else to do, but what is this haired thing and consciousness before me? What part of it matters, what is available? Why does so much depend on it in this moment? What is there to do about it? How can I make it allow me to be what I want toward it? I shiver in and out of longing and blank stupidity. Will she understand that what I want is what the moment is made of? Or will she make me nothing again? A pathetic and fake "help me" is wrung from the conglomeration of cells with my name and I focus and project it toward her, aim it at her, as if she could know, until that wears out in a second or two. I want to have my mouth on hers, put my dick inside her, etc. I am squirming in and out of this pinched delirium, cold and sad and hard-pressed. It seems like some last subterranean dead end, even the finality of which is false, where something is happening that no one is aware of—not even its participants, inhabitants, players, citizens, occupants, passengers, attendants: us. It seems hopeless and ironic that here beside and behind her I am suffering this minor crisis of loneliness and lust in the darkness without a witness, or even an inkling myself. It's a swirling world in my head that means nothing, not even to me, but nevertheless is familiar and awful. How can it not be real? I just want to hold her and have her let me, let me do what I will with her and welcome it, kiss me in return. Ugh.

I hate myself for depending on her to save me now. I know how futile and deluded it is. I scrunch up against her carefully, molding myself all along the back of her as smoothly and undisturbingly as I can and then when there is no protest, reach my upper arm around and rest the hand below her neck, against her sternum. She squirms a little as if she is irritated and I pull us together more tightly and try to lie there as if it is all natural. She squirms again and elbows me in the side. That can't be misinterpreted. I back off and in a moment get out of the bed and into mine.

30

Dreary. When morning comes we are like strangers. The day is gray again and I have to go through the bad little maze of arranging transportation for the DeSoto carcass. We call a taxi for a ride to the rental shop and pay a mechanic to return with us to the car to hook it up.

It's a small truck we're renting to pull the car over the Mississippi down through a corner of Indiana and across Western Kentucky to Lexington. All this abortion is degrading. It's not fun to navigate the concrete circa St. Louis in a moving van with a big useless old car swinging from its rear. I don't know how to deal with it except to hate it.

After a while though, once we are away from the city and I've gotten a little accustomed to the truck and into the rhythm of driving it isn't so bad.

In a few hours we cross the border into Kentucky and it immediately feels like Kentucky. This part of the state is cut-off, primitive, and alien. It's a thick and gorgeous wilderness far from civilization, where prickly little crawling pockets of the ignored hide to cultivate their ignorance, incest the preferred means. The back roads feel farther from homogenized America, from the world, than any we've driven. It feels dangerous.

It's a long drive from the western border to Lexington. Eventually, the ominous, beautiful hill country gives way to the more smoothly rolling farmland that's familiar to me, and then we're in among the immaculate horse farms with their white-washed plank fences marking off the famous rich grass of the lushest deep green, a green so deep, like the ocean, that later in the summer in the right light it can almost look blue. The sight of it, the sense of a familiarity deeper than the conscious, moves and excites me. It has me talking to Chrissa again.

The air smells good and the light is unbound. It makes me think of Saturday mornings after cartoons with all the potent grid of hilly streets that lead to specific houses and shops—the hobby shop where you could get models and toys or the pharmacy where you could sit at the counter and get a cheeseburger and syrupy sodas . . . Or hiding places in silent fields wherein are nestled our sparkling intense small voices. You'd need a stethoscope to hear them and still never again will they be understood except by another heart. The years since seem like badly constructed walls and hallways and façade that collapse at the slightest pressure. The landscape of Kentucky reopens into endless possibilities. Any moment is a beginning. What are we gonna do today? Let's run away.

How relative can innocence be, I wonder. Is being born itself a loss of it? I don't miss my childhood. I know it was as painful and confusing as the present. The interesting thing is how present it is and it is returning to where I was a child that brings it home.

Of course I am a depraved drug addict now, but it's all of a piece and the same yearnings and fears that I'd had as a kid have taken me here. Even if I were to succeed in stopping, the underlying impulse wouldn't go away. I'd just have to live with it, find other means of coping. I doubt if I could. All that "growing up" means is that if you are lucky you learn how better to cope with who you are—who you are doesn't change. In fact, that is probably the very definition of who one is—that which doesn't change. Living and identity are a kind of artform. You have this material—yourself—and the challenge is to explore or present it, to find a language and style for its display, its manifestation, that correspond to and are suited to tracking its nature. Anything seen in its fullness is beautiful. Or that's the only hope we have anyway.

Kentucky isn't exactly the South but it's more South than North. The accents have that twang, and the food is biscuits and gravy and chicken-fried steak and turnip greens. The music is bluegrass, just about the most cheerful sounding music to ever be filled with death, and archaic hill country wailing that sounds Elizabethan, otherworldly. It is rural, back-woodsy, and the people are peasants. I like that about it. It's funny—when we stop to eat I still respond to the personal threat and challenge offered by the hawing, swaggering teenage boys with their calloused grease-stained hands and their Camaros and pickup trucks, and I'm also determined to be admired by the girls with their big hairdos and soft starch-stuffed bellies and dimestore sweatclothes. I don't speak their language, of course. I come from a different class, and I'm self-conscious and neurotic, but I want them to accept me. I prefer them and their parents for company to the typical examples of the other native class—vulgar self-satisfied pretentious people who wear Ivy League imitation country squire button-downs and khakis and penny loafers and sneer at the others. Their ignorance is a much more obnoxious strain.

It's getting toward dark as we approach my hometown. Lexington is the second-biggest city in the state, ruled by a few out-of-state corporations and the tobacco industry, as well as the local old money who own the thoroughbred horse farms for which the area is famous. It's a college town, too, with a large state university and a smaller private college both in the center of the city.

When I was growing up it was a quiet, slow-moving place. The population was about a hundred thousand. That number has doubled since I left, and the outskirts of the place are now like the tacky edge of everywhere in the U.S., with the same clutter of fast-food franchises and rearing tangles of gawky chain-store emblems along the concrete lots and roads.

The bloodthirsty national merchants and the Chamber of Commerce have pretty well gutted the place I remember and taken and tucked the town's original character into the overall commercial park. The center of town, which when I was a kid hadn't changed much in the century, and was pleasingly time-worn and functional, has now either been torn down or renovated for artificial preservation as an example of itself.

Still, some remains. I call my aunt and get her directions to the garage where we are to leave the car, and as we drive the streets with names that have the remnants of strange childhood superstitions and associations attached to them, I feel this warm and ectoplasmic but detached surge of magical unreality, as if I've gotten lost in time. It doesn't seem possible that these places could still be here, unless I am a child.

The garage is closed but we unhitch the car and park the truck around beside it. In a moment, my aunt is there to take us to her house.

I've seen even less of my aunt than I have of the rest of the family in the thirteen years since I dropped out of high school and went to New York. She is my mother's little sister and is only nine years older than me. She is the last family member still in Kentucky. Her name is Janey.

I feel a little guilty toward her. My mother and my sister both adore her but I've always been her favorite. I know I can safely take her affection and fascination for granted and more than once when I was a kid I had her lie for me, which is really contrary to her nature.

She's always given a lot of time to her work with a local theater group and has always dreamed of being a professional actress, though she is really a high school teacher. She never got married and she's essentially proper in the old Southern tradition, but at the same time she has this naïve, clichéd conception of the exalted artiste who has the right to live by a separate code. She is a slightly formal, cheerful, very kind person who's actually thought of as sharp and acerbic, even cynically witty, down here, but it's a more primitive level of knowing wit than I'm used to in New York and I sometimes can't resist showing her up. She doesn't seem to mind. She is proud of me.

She is delighted to meet Chrissa and we all pile into her little car and head for her apartment. Arrogantly, but without afore-thought, it's hard for me to believe that she can have the values and dreams she has and still stay in this town. I have to guard against showing condescension. I keep having to restrain my tendency to speak of the place strictly anecdotally, as a finished and obvious closed book. I'll suddenly remember that she is still living here and have to change my tone as smoothly as I can.

She lives along one of the leafy old residential streets not far from the university, on the top floor of a two-story house. The woman who owns the building lives downstairs and has made over the upper floor as an apartment by putting in a kitchen and sealing off access from below. Jane graciously, tactfully, offers whatever arrangement we want to make between the little second bedroom and a foldout couch in the living room and Chrissa immediately makes it clear we'll be using them both.

We've arrived on a Thursday night and my aunt has to work the next day but then she'll have the weekend off. I tell her I am expecting a package tomorrow. Chrissa gives me a look that Aunt Jane doesn't miss. I put on a record and we sit around the living room sipping bourbon and talking.

My aunt is really an angel, but I get this forgotten familiar uncomfortable feeling after the initial warmth wears off a little, because she makes me feel like a predator. She just likes me too much and that is dangerous. Later in the evening when I am in the bathroom I check the medicine cabinet. Sure enough there is an old prescription bottle with seven or eight percodans left in it. I've scored. These will hold me till at least Sunday if the dope doesn't come tomorrow. I feel like Superman.

3 1

The next morning Janey has a friend pick her up to take her to work so she can leave Chrissa and me the car. She says the mail will come at around 11:00.

I swallow a couple of the big percodans. It's the first time in a while that the morning feels like a morning. The giant trees shading the street outside and the homey, spooky old two- and three-story wooden houses behind them look mythological and hood-eyed with secrets. Meanwhile the belieing air enters everywhere, softly, like a discreet and sexy servant, freshening with its incidence of new-mown grass and sweetest water.

I stall around, drinking coffee, talking and reading the local newspaper until the mailman comes. He doesn't have my package.

Chrissa and I drive out for breakfast. We find a steamy little storefront diner on the edge of downtown a few blocks away. The waitresses are hillbillies. The menu is mimeographed and includes that delicious salty country ham and homemade biscuits with redeye gravy. There are also pies named after whoever's recipe was behind them. I get ham and eggs and Chrissa gets Tammy's Precious Pecan Pie with a scoop of vanilla ice cream. "Can I hot that up for you, darlin?" Pretty soon Chrissa is chatting with half the restaurant about the differences between Paris, France, and Paris, Kentucky.

I want to drive over and check out the suburb where I grew up while all the residents are still at work or in school. Chrissa is having such a good time where she is we decide we'll just meet up back at the house later. There's an extra key outside under the steps.

It's just as well I'm driving out to Gardenside solo. I want a pure reaction to it. I've gotten directions from Janey or I'd have a hard time finding it. All the distances seem shorter and my child-simple mental map of the town excludes whole districts and what remains seems half-erased.

As I get nearer, every block and view is more intensely eerie, with subtle residues of lingering character and tones of emotional intimation resident to them. There is more mess—not many of the open spaces of my childhood remain—but most of the streetscape is powerfully familiar in this strange distorted way that it has inherited from our long-gone intimacy.

I find the street where I grew up. I drive by my house and then park the car out of the way and get out and walk. There is no one on the streets and I slowly realize I am a ghost. I'm genuinely insubstantial because my mind is making me up on this street that is indubitably real. I am in two times at once and it has the effect of vaguing me physically in them both. It doesn't know me but I know it. Walking isn't like walking; it's a kind of managed drifting. I am scanning, I am moving some kind of mechanism with my mind that draws the street past me. All of me is thinned through.

The street is utterly ordinary: forlorn in that way. It is a completely typical, barren, predesigned fifties suburban street. Nothing is distinctive about it—not only is it just like the streets on both sides of it, but there are only three different house designs on the block. Mine is the plainest. I've never realized it before but it actually is a perfect representation of a child's idea of a house: a little box with a door centered between the two front windows, topped by one peaked angle of roof. There is even a little chimney on one side. The street stretches up a hill and every house has a yard that slopes fifty feet down to the sidewalk and then a hundred feet to the lot behind. Along the right side of each is a driveway a few paces from the building next door. Each front yard contains two trees so isolated in their symmetrical placement smack in the centers of the rectangles made by the houses' front walkways that they still look scrawny and inept after all these years.

It's as if my vision is weak, or that the picture I'm looking at is blurred, stretched and pulled across the interval of time, so that the grain is hopelessly enlarged. It's all there but dominated by the void between the particles of faded-out color. Still, I am walking in it, it's real. I feel incredibly alone but comfortable in it, as if I have the God's-eye view. I reach down and pick up a pebble and throw it up the street, and that act seems brave, a stupendous display of initiative.

There is no one around at all. I go and stand across the street from my house and look at it. I know the house really has nothing itself, that I am investing it with any power it has, and that if I abuse that power it will collapse, shrink, and get ugly. I turn and start back down the street.

I walk and drive in this strange pocket of ur-time. I would like to re-mark, to physically return upon, the topology in time of the entire topography of my prior existence in this place. To recover every distant step for what it might release, caught in this fragile trance of supreme receptivity, and to reclaim it. It would be interesting to be that thorough, but it would be insane and self-defeating. I'm not quite that obsessively fascinated by my childhood. I know that it's ordinary and that there isn't much of use to be learned in the nauseating effort to revivify it. It's the new mental state created by the place that is marvelous and it has to be cultivated with some delicacy.

It is nourishing and private, a kind of audience with God. A view of the way things are. It isn't really joining me to my life but separating me into the everlasting.

I roam around, rolling on tires I can hear slowly flap against the asphalt, and savor tiny sips of the details pouring through the windshield for a couple of hours. Whenever my mind, under the influence of all these signals, drifts into the state where I find myself half and quizzically groping, distractedly grasping and extending to reenter my psychology, my consciousness, my experience as a nine- or ten-year-old or a fourteen-year-old, I veer away so as not to break the spell. It is something you can only get at all by not directly going for it, like the location and velocity of an electron or like a gift in a fairy tale that has conditions attached. Mostly what is still available is love and ennui, run through with a little fear and anger and bewilderment, and this desire to explode and diffuse and break free that seems sad in its futility, in its human smallness, in its egotism, in its loneliness. There is a big open space that has a kind of chill to it, and somewhere, among many, but ignorantly and isolated from them, as is the rule, is one bright kink among the limitless crepuscular, one more particular little livingdying concentration of energy and that is me at seven years old. Entropy is the rule. It is pretty though.

It is great to be inside a map of evocative surprises. A kind of mental Christmas. I drive the streets of houses that remind me of childhood friends, past the shopping center, the school, the playground, a few welcome overgrown still-undeveloped areas, cross and recross a stream that winds through, until I finally become uncertain and a little bored, my processing capacities dulled. I turn away and start back toward downtown.

32

I drive around the town center, which has become far more misshapen and recustomized by time than my suburb, get a little something to eat, and go back to my aunt's.

Chrissa isn't there. I maturely postpone taking another percodan, and sit upstairs facing a window, a glass of whiskey and my notebook at my side.

Aunt Jane ought to be back from work in about an hour. I am glad to be alone. Her apartment is nice. I bet the boys in her classes are crazy about her. I start to get fond and cozy thinking about her. I go into her bedroom and open her drawers and look at her clothes and then I find her laundry hamper and pull out some of her panties and bras and look at them and smell them. That deglamorizes us both pretty well, but it's nice underwear. Abruptly, I drop them back and return to the living room.

What am I doing? I don't know. Sometimes it gets like that, where some unexamined, nonintellectual part of you turns on and takes over and you just go, with seeming, with deceptive, nondeliberation, where it leads. You don't want to think, you don't want to know, because you might miss something really good and interesting if you interfere out of scruples, and you don't even think about that decision. This is probably what people mean by the devil. I feel like poetic Superman again, the Hamlet of Krypton, that I have inhuman power and no restraints, that my latitude breaks all boundaries. I am a Hamlet who drifts on blood, dizzy, like a drunken boat, and though I might brood, the blood will inevitably move me, will take me where it goes, and I like it. I like that weakness that saves me from my weakness by making me weaker. Weak, like wake and sleep, like weep. I smile to myself like a wolf and take another drink.

Before long I hear Aunt Jane being dropped off outside. When she comes in the door and sees me she smiles the most open, radiant, pleasure-filled recognition. It's amazing that something so silent can be so dramatic and something so dramatic be so innocent, so generous. I've forgotten I can have that effect on a person. She not only has faith in me but she trusts me.

"Hi, nephew."

That sounds false. She means an intimacy, but "nephew" doesn't have a meaning to me; she is drawing on an empty account and she doesn't even know it. It makes me feel superior again; that I have greater resources in the interchange between us.

I get up to help her with the grocery bags she's carrying. "Hi Aunt Jane." Saying those words as I walk toward her and her face and body enlarge and enlarge in my vision, I realize they do have a meaning, but one that only exists as specialized equipment, like a sex toy. Her face is flushed and bright, with emerging sweat droplets at the hairline. Maybe I'll kill her. Just kidding.

"Where's Chrissa?"

"I'm not sure. I bet she's taking pictures. I left her with some hillbillies in a diner this morning while I went out to Gardenside."

"You did?"

"It was her idea. I think she saw some art in it."

"She's wonderful. You always have such pretty, nice, creative girlfriends."

"The better to eat you with."

"What?"

I don't know. I laugh. "I don't know. I don't know what the fuck that was. Oops. Sorry. What I'm saying."

"It's OK Billy. You can be yourself with me."

"Really?"

"Of course."

"That's offering a lot."

"I hope not. I hope you always feel that way with me."

"But I'm a kind of a fucked-up person, Janey."

"Who isn't? But not all of us can write poems the way you do."

"I don't really write poems."

"What do you mean?"

"I don't know. Never mind. Look at this food . . ."

We're in the kitchen starting to put the groceries away. It takes strength not to hear myself with disgust. She's bought fancy things at the supermarket, including all the things she remembers as my favorites. In a minute she is making a plate with bread and crackers and some Roquefort and Brie and Italian olives and creamy pink caviar spread and she's even gotten smoked oysters. She has a couple of bottles of wine, too, and I open one and pour us some.

"Tell me what you've been up to," I say.

"Well, I just played Amanda Wingfield in *The Glass Menagerie* . . ."

"That's the mother?"

"Yes. The delusional, overbearing mother. I'm doing mothers now."

"You look absolutely great."

"Thank you, Billy."

"You really do. You look like you're pregnant or something," I say, embarrassing us both a little. "I mean, just the glow on you. Do you go running?"

"I dance, but, no, I'm just happy to see you."

"You're not pregnant, you're just happy to see me?"

She drinks some wine. She doesn't know what to say. I manage to maintain an appearance of confidence without really knowing much what is going to come out of my mouth next.

"Let's take this in the living room," she says. "What was it like in Gardenside?"

We carry the tray and glasses into the front room.

"It was really weird. It was like returning to the scene of the crime . . . or going to a place where everyone had died. My mind didn't know who—or when—I was. I was like a ghost. But it was interesting. It was cool, I liked it."

"Are you going to write about it?"

"I guess so. I don't know. Some way or another. That's what the trip is about, but I don't know if that was the right kind of stuff. It's got to go with Chrissa's pictures. You ought to see her pictures. You wanna see them? I've got some here."

"Sure. I'd love to," she says, finishing her glass of wine. "Let me go change out of these school-teacher clothes."

I fetch the set of pictures Chrissa has given me from my bags while Janey goes to change. I refill her wineglass. In a minute she comes back in faded jeans and an old-fashioned ring-collared white blouse. I go to the bathroom and swallow another big percodan.

She sits next to me on the couch and I can smell her perfume. I'm nervous and I drink some more. My mouth feels dry. I wonder if she has any idea of the electricity I feel from her. I feel so much bigger than her, strictly physically. I am. It makes me want to envelop her. I hope she will keep drinking. She takes another sip of her wine. I'd like to hold her head back by the hair and pour some down her throat. In a friendly way.

We look at the pictures. Do I have her or not? Will she submit? Can I get what I want from her? How do I find out without spoiling the outcome? I can hardly breathe. I feel like a kid on his first date. My face is a pomegranate, my lungs are rocks, and my dick is next door stuffing itself at table like a cartoon fake of a crazy murderer.

That moment passes and I have the sense of engulfing her now and I feel immense. I have the incalculable distance from her of an ocean in which she is suspended, half-sunken. It never occurs to her that I know she is there, in me, at my mercy. I look at her with infinite cold solicitude and certainty. I am the great villain but I am human and I love her. I want to suck her nipples and put my tongue in her asshole. With love. I want to come on her face, I want to swallow her innards, because it will make her feel so good. I'll do it worshipfully. She'll scream with the ecstasy. She'll be so surprised, my aunt. She ought to know, she ought to learn about this. It'll be good for her. We'll like it.

I put some old Motown on the record player. We are both cheerful and happy looking at the pictures and continuing to drink.

She marvels at the pictures and they serve my purposes. They frighten her a little while also making her feel a part of an exciting larger world and these things tend to accelerate her drinking.

We talk about the pictures and I tell her about the stages I've gone through in trying to figure out what to write for them and it is clear that, casual as she tries to appear, she is flattered to be included among the aesthetic cognoscenti, the cosmopolitans. It has gotten cloudy gray outside and now it is getting dark.

Sitting by her on the couch I reach a breaking point and in a kind of spaced way, feeling as if I am almost fainting, I reach out and put my hand around her waist. It is incredibly strange and intimate to feel her hipbone and belly beneath her blouse, and it's like death. She turns to face me with a small look of innocent delight and gratitude for the sweet moment with her nephew. I pull her upper body towards me and the expression on her face crumbles as I move my head down and kiss her on the mouth. Her mouth is even better than her belly.

33

I have my eyes closed as I stick my tongue in her mouth. It only lasts for a split second but my God, her mouth is like a furnace; prehistoric, molten grown-up candy. Heart-stopping, a perfect fit. I can feel it in my nipples. Shared genes winking at each other. Incredibly hot.

Then we pull back and she's looking at me in stricken confused amazement. Her face is bright pink and I am red, too, but I also have this confidence in achievement, this feeling of control, of arrival at a great new peak. I am a skilled and decisive, trustworthy leader. She seems to have become younger than me.

"Billy. What are you doing?"

"Feeling really good."

"You can't do that."

"Why? Didn't you like it?" I rasp, despite my thrill of control, my choked voice husky and breathless.

She pauses. "Am I really supposed to think about that?" And I know I have her.

"No, don't think. Just come with me." I stand up, holding her hand. She stands up.

"Where?" she asks, a little stupidly. Jesus, it all feels exalted and inevitable, destiny grinding. I kiss her again. I am so much bigger than her. Wider especially, but the previous generation in our family wasn't all that tall. Assured as I am, kissing her still takes my breath away. Her tongue responds again for a moment and it feels so correct and fantastic, so light and piercing. Then I reach for the wine bottle and start leading her toward her bedroom.

"Billy, we have to talk."

"I want to see you with your clothes off."

She blushes again. I pour some wine in myself.

"Did you always want to do this?" she asks.

"Yes, I must have. I don't know," I say. Doesn't everyone?

"I should stop you. I don't want to. I've never wanted to stop you . . ." She's referring to how protective and solicitous she'd always been, defending me . . .

We are in the bedroom now, but she is holding herself a little off from me. The way she is thinking about it and clinging to being my older aunt is irritating, and then it also seems like she might be becoming coy like any girl and I hate that. Couldn't she just see how cool it is? I shove the bottle of wine at her and she lifts it to her lips and guzzles some which makes everything sexy and pleasurable again. As she drinks I undo the top of her jeans.

"Billy, I can't let go. I'm sorry. This is insane. Is it really what you want to do?"

It is too late for me. I feel for a second the idea that I could cut it short here, but it is too late. Not only are my systems past the point of no return, but it would be such an embarrassment and a psychological waste to stop. We'd have all the grim residue of the act without its substance. It is almost mechanical, but I pull her through it. We are both pretty drunk. I don't love her, of course, whatever love is—I guess I should say I have no romantic feelings toward her, though it is fun to pretend them a little to myself. It is just something I think I'll be allowed, I physiologically am adequately stimulated to do, and that seems like it would be an interesting thing to have done.

In the process I get cocky, as if we are taunting God with our transgression, flaunting our freedom, and she picks this up where it mixes in her with a kind of desperation to avoid thinking about what is really going on. While, as always, something about her is beyond me—I don't really "get" her—she's a mystery like everyone. It is so trashy and nice and ego-inflating to have my hard cock in my sweet aunt. My self-regard is swollen like a balloon inside my skull and though there are little bats and dark winds whistling and flittering around outside of it and squashed against the bone in places, they don't make much of an impression. They can't begin to penetrate the enormous fat ego. Or maybe it's love.

The whole thing happens in a squall, in a violent little storm on her big soft bed, once it gets started. How great to know her body that way. The sense of the subliminally known, the subconsciously extrapolated, the beyond-limits-but-secretly-suspected, the daydream come true, come owned, come known. It is magical, twisted, and stunning. We are in another world. And she has an amazingly tight and clinging vagina for a woman her age. She must not have had much sex.

I don't know if I want to look her in the eyes anyway—yes I do—but I am safe because she keeps them closed. I look at her everywhere else. As I lick and jam my lips and tongue up into her cunt I press my hard cock against her hairless calf. Even her crotch, which maybe in my whole life I have glimpsed once for a second as a child, seems so close, so known, while also lathered with all that sexiness, the control she is ceding me. It is soft and tender and the hair is silky and it smells so sweet. I hold her still-firm butt in both hands and push apart the crack and lick her asshole, too. But I am like a dog with this red-hot cock that I just want to imprint against every inch of her body. And I love kissing her. It is the only point at which she has to take a really overtly active part and in her exquisitely reticent way she does. It is as if she really loves me. She joins in the deep kisses with a kind of tentative expanding abandon, starting in tenderness and ending where the world does and unjudging—and though shy, willing to enjoy them for all they are worth. Her face is burning. She is exploding. Once I have my cock inside her I get a little scared. I want to stop time. It feels so good and where will we be when it is over? I am so turned on I'm afraid I'll come immediately, but the substances and my fear itself seem to be working to make it last. She starts to come! God, that is great. It is all going to work out perfectly, like a fairy tale. She is making noises she can't restrain as I kiss and suck on her mouth and neck and breasts and fuck her hard. I am beatific as my long fat cock starts stuttering droplets and then flinging gobs of gush deep up into her when the real silent explosions start. I turn my head and my semiconscious eyes seem to catch something hulking at the doorway.

I gasp and my doubled mind shudders insanely and leaps back toward itself, missing, and hurls itself back again, with my heart on a length of gristle swerving crazily in the air three feet behind it and I almost die of ferocious fear, brain frantically groping to classify while my gyrating heart turns black-green and my blood paining metal. Even when I recognize Chrissa, the killer is still there, and the needles penetrating my body keep sliding through horribly and my whole head and face are swollen and it won't stop. She has a camera to her eye and has started clicking off flash pictures. What?!? Flooding influxes of embarrassment mixed with panic and roaring new streams of anger, and I don't know what I am doing. God damn her. My head swivels back down toward Aunt Janey. My groan and the interruption in my rhythm has gotten her attention and now she opens her eyes, but I am rearing above her and she can't see that Chrissa is there yet. I realize I've spontaneously drawn my soaking cock full back out of her. She looks at me bewildered and she must see not just the freakish emotion for which she can have no explanation but the thing in my eyes that I'd avoided faking as otherwise but didn't want her to see and that now is really something more and else altogether: That I don't know her at all and don't care to. A sadness and fear I'll never be able to reach passes across the erotically charged-up surface of her face and I don't even really notice. She makes a terrible small effort to ask me something, as I, still in the clutch of a single drawn-out reaction flop away to the side like a fish, my smelly, wasted, withering cock dangling behind. Camera flashes popping off capture my aunt's unbearable confusion and horror as she finally sees Chrissa and jolts and screams. I am crouched up like a preying monkey behind and above her, frozen but gorged with adrenalin.

They both start saying things, Chrissa cold and angry and Janey hysterical, broken, crying. I leap over the mattress to attack Chrissa, shouting "Get out of here! Get the fuck out of here!" and she steps back flashing a few more pictures without even lifting the camera, as if it were a weapon. I make a swipe at the camera, and then I push her and she doesn't fight but just stumbles back awkwardly, awry like a rag doll from the force of it and I suddenly feel as uncertain and terrible as I ever have in my life to see her vulnerability and how it's unsafe with me. She turns around and leaves the room and all I can do is close the door behind her. The irredeemable hopelessness and ridiculousness of my position is starting to gain on my fury. I turn back toward my aunt who has her back to me, curled up, gasping and weeping. I move in that direction and sit on the edge of the bed feeling way too undressed. "Go away," she says. I sit there trembling, completely exposed.

I hear Chrissa leave through the front door.

34

Then it occurs to me that she might even think that I've set this up with Chrissa.

"Aunt Jane, Aunt Jane, you don't think I had anything to do with that, do you? She's crazy. She can't use them or anything—it would be illegal . . ." As I'm speaking I realize how crazy it is of me to think it possible that Jane could imagine I've arranged all this, and further how pathetic it is that this is what I have to say to her at this moment. Then I think I'm really not so sure about what Chrissa might want to do with the pictures. I freak, completely disoriented, without a clue about what's taken place . . .

I lean toward my quietly sobbing aunt and touch her back and say, "I'm sorry—"

She withdraws from my hand as if it burns. "Please leave me alone. Just go away."

I hear my voice and its banal and cheap self-preserving purposes in this moment following when time should have stopped.

"Could I go into the living room?" It's so strange how one can see with perfect clarity the falseness in how one is behaving at a given moment but be unable to behave any differently. The world should have split open by now.

After another moment, she says, "Yes, all right."

I pick up my clothes and take them into the living room and put them on and sit in a chair. My glass of whiskey is still there.

I can't believe I am still alive. It is my punishment not to die. Fuck shit piss. What can I do to make this better? Hit my head against the wall? Jump out the window? It's only two stories high. What kind of world and life is it where I can behave like this, be like this and survive to sit and sip whiskey in the living room? Argh. Who am I now? And where? It's exciting. Just who

I want to be and where I want to go. Apparently . . . obviously. The fucking look on her face. I keep coming back, stunned and blank, at one remove from profoundest self-loathing. Listening to myself say, *Please kill me.* Man, it is some bad fun.

You do the drugs, have the sex, and there's no dignity in it. I don't want to be human. I hate hate hate this being human. I'm not up to it, I can't . . . How do people do it? Jesus fucking piss shit cunt *aghk*.

Aunt Jane stays in her bedroom.

I am consigned to this place. It is my fate. Character is destiny. I keep drinking.

After a while, just to do something, in search of escape, I kind of furtively get out my books and try to read them. Every time I hear a stirring in the bedroom I freeze and tune to it like a wild deer. I am a little nervous about what she would think if she caught me calmly reading. I wish I was in a motel room. Or back home. I do consider going to knock on her door and try to do something for her, but I am comfortable and she knows I am here. I don't want to interfere. Oh shit.

What a cool thing, to sleep with your mother's sister. That is some information, something to flesh out the identity. Now it is time to move on to something else.

Time passes.

I look down at my left arm. There it is. What is it? It doesn't lead anywhere. It attaches to my shoulder. My shoulder leads up to here, where it gets lost. The only thing left is my nose, a kind of blur, and the very top of my cheek, and my upper lip if I stick it out. My left arm, there in such clarity. I suppose it has two states, on or off. Binary. Alive or not. No, I don't know, is there a difference? I move it. I can make it do things, but still it is just something folded into the air, it is no different than anything else. Nothing's inert. What fucking difference does it make what the fuck I do? I'm not real, I'm not separate, I'm just a bundle of impulses of greater or lesser strength bouncing around the chamber until it all leads down the drain, where it pools, evaporates, condenses, rains, pools, while something clicks in another tunnel and another battered node emerges to swirl down the drain again. This is undeniable but uninteresting. I don't want to be seduced by the interesting though, I want to know what the fuck is really happening and I want to live with it, I want to live in it. Fuck fuck fuck.

Maybe I can break the cycle in a snap, like a toothpick, by doing something contrary. Something impossible, something outside the bargain. But that's where my music career came from, I think, and I saw that it just got swallowed by the world where it became another inevitability. It's a delusion to think you can outsmart who you are and what you must do. Well, it's time to move on. You just have to stay alert and keep moving.

I search for some guilt in myself about what I've done with my aunt and Chrissa. The search itself is an act of guilt and I do feel like a worm, but I am glad, too. It is kind of exhilarating in a pinched and lonely, vicious way. I am free again. I am beyond sad.

It's as if I look at myself and project on emotions the way one will with an animal—a cat. The animal causes a significant accident and great drama to happen and it makes no impression whatsoever on the creature and its permanent expression; the cat is uninvolved, its sphere is elsewhere, but helplessly one gives some kind of value to that, one reads some kind of personality into the cat and its indifference, and then one realizes this is unrealistic and then something seems cold and evil and something seems sad and . . .

Somewhere I am in a back room crying, crying and crying like a little boy who's just realized in one instant what it means for something to die, because something he really loved is dead, and he is responsible for killing it; it died because he wasn't good enough, he's failed to care for it properly, but I can not face that door. I can damn well go on forever and not face that door. Some day it will open, or maybe it won't, but I am not going to walk back there. Aow, the pain, it is awful and fuck it. Time to move on.

Where is the grace? I know there are those who have it. I love them. And generally if given the opportunity I will hurt them. Ugh. Where is the grace? I want it. I want what will make it possible for me to help Janey now, but I have no idea, I'm not up to it, I don't have the humility, the desirable thoughtless thoughtfulness, my heart and mind just flounder and I am worthless. Somebody help me, please. I don't have the resources. Can God help me? How can I console her when I'm the offender?

I'm not seeing the pages I am trying to read. I keep looking up with these thoughts shooting through my head, my heart reaching and groping convulsively. And then I write a line in my notebook. I wonder if I can pray. I know God doesn't care. That God is simply the way things are. But I also know that something in me knows what is right. Even if "right" is only that which is consistent with some peace of mind, for all of us, that which is consistent with an egoless flow, not broken by misbegotten, willful interruptions, by egotistic arguments and assertions, human misinterpretations and twisted intellectual interference, for all of us. But wasn't I acting with that flow when I was kissing her? Agh, it is hopeless, I am out of my depth.

I start to try to pray, just to find some quiet, just to find the place where prayer has a meaning. I pray for help to know how to pray for help to know how to help. I get glimpses, but it is useless. God, the fucking pain. All I can do is look at myself and feel disgust. It is all false. I'm not going to do anything. I don't know how to change.

The pain is like a wire squeezing, my heart grotty and garroted. I think I will go crazy. I want to scream but I know I can't. And it is all so pathetic. My ego going around in circles till it makes itself nauseous. But wouldn't going to Jane just be that much more presumptuous? Shut up shut up shut up. I feel suicidal. This situation is horrifyingly recognizable. I can't possibly try to recall what has taken me here before, but the sense that who I am is what leads to this is ineluctable and excruciating. All this squirming and fucking writhing, it isn't living anyway. I am dizzy, fucking dizzy with the pain. Please kill me. But even suicide is some kind of self-congratulation, a lie. Do it or shut up. I know I won't do it. There are always drugs, and anyway I am too curious about what will happen next. Death is already going to happen, so you'll find out about that.

Guilt is so boring and meaningless. I decide to get up and go outside. I write a note to Aunt Jane telling her I've gone for a walk and will be back soon. Just in case she comes back out. I put the whiskey bottle in a bag and take it with me.

It is drizzling out in the dark, it's wet. It is warm and wet. It smells good. Widely spaced streetlights along the big-treed avenue give it a cozy warmth and security that repels and angers me. It is so damned self-sufficient and unreachable. The warmth is bone cold. I am vertiginous with the outpouring of tainted self-conscious atmosphere from inside me infecting and stripping the surroundings, but worse having no effect on them at all. It is nauseating and it makes me want to kill or break something, to cringe in the mute face of it. I hope the whiskey will soften the effect. I lower down into a crouch on the balls of my feet in the rain in the darkness in front of the house. A car cruises past and my hatred is overwhelming. The indifference of it is too much to tolerate. I am drinking from the bottle. I throw it at the car. It nicks the fender without breaking and slides spinning in the street. The car slows to a stop and two burly young guys get out and check the car, looking around. I am deeply terrified. Is this going to be taken out of my hands now? But I don't move and they get back in the car and drive off. Oh fuck, now I don't have anything to drink. I go and retrieve the bottle and there is only a half inch left in the bottom. I take it back to the yard. Shit, I can't even get myself properly beat up. I think, I bet if somebody was watching I would have taunted those guys . . . What a fucked-up life. I need some god damned thing. I sit in the grass beneath a tree and it soaks my pants. I lie in it on my back and suck the last drops from the bottle. Things look kind of interesting from here, the starry sky blocked by invisible leaves and all, but I'm getting really wet. I feel self-conscious and in a moment I get up and walk back to the house. I hesitate near the steps and turn around to start toward the yard again. Then I turn and half-step back toward the house, then I swivel on my heels around again like a puppet and I stand there for a minute in the rain, furious and empty and pathetic and then almost laughing before I climb up and go inside.

35

Next day. I don't feel so good. Now if I was really cut out to be a performer, I'd just get lost or kill something now. Cover or transform my weakness with mystery or a blaze. But I don't have enough drugs to care or not care or whatever it is. I don't have enough drugs to exist.

Let me tell you, it just gets worse.

I remember one time I took too much THC. For four or five hours in the deadest part of night I lay as still as I could, alone on a bed in a lit-up room. The horror was that the overdose gave this *significance*, this meaningful message, you know what I'm talking about, to everything whatsoever *and to each thing to the same degree.* Smoking a joint times ten million. To God is one thing more important than another? I have never been so scared for so long. I felt like I was dead because there was no me to assert in the face of all this, but at the same time I would continually disgust myself with inescapable conclusions about my character as revealed in its pathetic, suspicious, spontaneous reactions to all phenomena. I was nothing but reflexes and all the universe was unknowing. I just wanted everything to stop happening. I was so wide open there was no distance, no protection, between me and all of it. I'd close my eyes for relief and I'd be emptiness hurtling through the random emptiness, battered by aggressively ominous stray sounds and smells, the awfulness of which clearly originated in me. Like a permanent continuous disaster, a terrible accident like a car wreck that just continued and continued. I was everything and everything was me and it was completely pointless and lonely at best, and heartbreaking in its exposure of my hopeless, final ugliness and insignificance at worst. Life an extended fatal accident.

What is the best one can hope for? It's so small. Shouldn't one rebel against one's smallness? To be humble and quiet may be spiritually healthy, to understand that everything is exactly as it should and must be, that to resist it is clearly self-defeating may be most wise, but don't you just want to mix it up a little bit? Don't you want to have an effect? Oh, mercy.

Chrissa I know can take care of herself. She's been through enough not to be vulnerable to serious pain from me anymore.

My aunt is another matter (though no doubt I'm underestimating her). She never would have fucked me at all if I hadn't gotten her drunk, and she never would have drunk like that if I hadn't kind of tricked her into it, using my unfair advantages. And now the next day I want to hold her to console her . . . ha!

I've known constricted, bitter people, people who feel they've lost and been cheated, who unconsciously take every opportunity to create experiences for those around them that will teach these others the same things they've so painfully learned. Am I like that? Was I betraying my aunt in order to show her that no one can be trusted? God help me.

God, she was a great fuck. For the likes of me. It was that dewy, open-faced, shy sweetness, combined with intelligence and unaffectedness. It's kind of amazing that she could live for as long as she has and maintain that spirit. You don't often get a chance like that, to dazzle and seduce a sweet and pretty near-virginal thirty-nine-year-old who knew you as a baby and is also your mother's sister. But it all just gets erased the moment it is seen from without; it is ruined.

Now I know where religions come from. Fear and self-hatred. It's too miserable to live not only aware of one's defects but of how none of it matters anyway.

Any kind of mission, any kind of drive to manipulate things to one's idea of what they should be is a sickness. All it does is reflect yourself while wearying and wounding, it doesn't make any difference. But life is a sickness. Some kind of infection of the inanimate. God is only the way things are, but God does have a will. It's called inertia. Things don't want to change. The larger thrust will not be altered. Rilke said the only battles worth living for are the unwinnable ones, the ones with angels. It is oneself that changes, one finds, and that is how the world is changed.

Stories are prophecies and they comfort with meaning. To tell what happened is to manipulate it into sense, reduce the loneliness and indicate direction, cut a person's grooves more deeply. They pass the time with time and make it beautiful and interesting, if only by removing it from context, where everything becomes interesting in its strangeness. Hearing a story is telling it is to be implicated in it.

It's fun to think. An interesting kind of hobby, but you've got to use a little restraint or you'll bore everybody to death and miss the action.

I don't want to reassure, to comfort artificially, to give the good lie to me or anyone else. But see, even that impulse to not be falsely neat is just my nature, it's not the truth. I will do what I have to do and no amount of thinking, no amount of considering the options has any meaning, it's merely characteristic, too. I want to give up. How can I give up? I want to give up.

The next morning is strange and uncomfortable. It is obvious that Aunt Jane wants and needs some kind of interpretation of what has happened, but there is no way it can be discussed. She tiptoes around the house, addressing me politely and quietly when necessary, but never looks me in the eyes. The atmosphere is of deep, not-cute, unglamorous, embarrassment and hurt and unasked questions. I am mildly hungover and worried about running out of narcotics. I took too many yesterday. I want to be home.

Chrissa calls eventually and we have a stiff conversation. She isn't planning on seeing me again. She's spoken to Jack who's decided to cut his losses and she's already booked herself a flight back to New York. The first available plane leaves in three days. She agrees to give me the plane fare to use as I will. I figure to take a train or bus and use the change drug-hunting.

All is unresolved. I want to forget it. What will we do for a book? Well, the car broke down. The book's been aborted by an act of God. I think I can make something out of what's actually happened but I don't know if Chrissa will tolerate collaborating with me any further. It is too much to think about, and as always the first order of business is finding narcotics. Aah, to hell with this.

Knowledge is like money; no matter how much you learn, no matter how much you earn, you are still yourself and exactly as close to the edge as where you began. You take for granted what you have and you can't take it with you. There's never enough, if you ever want any more you will always want more, no matter what you get. But you can't take it with you. When you die. And you die now. You die now. And all you can ever learn is what you already know.

What is left is a bruise.

"Dear God . . ."

One's capacity for forgetting one's failures and defects, one's fate . . .

We know what happens: more of the same.

Still, you always want to know what the ending is, but you can't, because you're dead.

Under a highway overpass for shelter in the rain. Somehow the money ran out. I am mystified. That "I" sounds wrong.

I'm on my knees before you. The words are on their knees. This dull, stunned dimwit. With his brain whirring. He's probably going to laugh. Ready to go. All the words. All the words since the beginning of time. The ending is words. The person in a cloud of them, like a cloud of bugs.

Step back, the person is emerging, elsewhere, emerging like a creature from a dead carapace or cocoon or a penis from a foreskin to resume his life outside our observation. The deformations he suffered for being inaccurately described are shuffled off.

That would be me.

The heat came on for the first time since spring this morning. It has that comforting smell it has every time it comes on again for the first time in the fall. I think it's the dust in the system burning off. It makes me feel at peace, and prepared for whatever may come. The methadone I just took doesn't hurt either.

As for the book, I'm going to write it. Or maybe I'm not. I did some speed and wrote two chapters, but I don't know where to take it from there. The trip was an abortion. I'd have to make it up. That's a lot of work.

The way things are now, a few bags of dope make me feel lucky. And you know I think it's true. I've always been lucky.

Printed in the United States
By Bookmasters